10 €

Círculo Rojo

To Wander Alone

To Wander Alone

Giles Powell

Círculo Rojo
EDITORIAL

Primera edición: junio 2018

Depósito legal: AL 1222-2018

ISBN: 978-84-9194-480-5

Impresión y encuadernación: Editorial Círculo Rojo

Editorial Círculo Rojo

www.editorialcirculorojo.com

info@editorialcirculorojo.com

Impreso en España - Printed in Spain

El papel utilizado para imprimir este libro es 100% libre de cloro y por tanto, **ecológico**.

In loving memory of the 'Best Mum.'

SUMMER

1
The Manila Envelope

Richard had considered meeting the courier in 'a neutral zone' such as the Victoria and Albert Museum or Earl's Court tube station but after some deliberation, he decided it was best to keep things simple. So he told the company to make the delivery direct to the Brownlowe Gallery.

The morning of the delivery, he was fidgety: he loosened his tie and undid the top button of his shirt. He drank three cups of coffee. Jean, his PA, had been given the day off so he logged into the computer at her desk, which looked out onto the King's Road, and checked his emails. Then he browsed the latest issue of a quarterly arts magazine.

Back then, during that summer, the gallery was housing sixteen portraits. The work of a group of contemporary artists from the UK. But the reviews had been terrible. Only one painting had sold. Richard looked up at that purchased image. It was oil on canvas, of an immigrant curled up on a London street. The title: Lost.

He stared through the gallery window. Outside, the heavens had opened and rain pelted the busy road where people were scurrying. What news will the delivery bring? Richard wondered. But he didn't want to think about it because the whole thing was making him nervous so he turned back to the quarterly arts magazine. There was an article about Van Gogh. The article questioned whether the Dutchman had really cut his own ear off in the French town of Arles in 1888. Couldn't someone else have done the injury? Paul Gaugin, perhaps? And what had become of the ear?

When the door bell sounded, Richard looked up to see a courier standing outside the door in the rain. She was holding a manila envelope. He rose to release the security lock. She pushed open the door and walked brusquely in. She was dripping wet and smelled of damp leather.

"Richard Brownlowe?" she asked.

"Correct," he said.

"You're paying in cash, right?"

He nodded, taking out a wad of money from the inside pocket of his jacket. It was the second and final payment for what Richard knew had been an illegal investigation. The courier slowly counted the money.

"Two grand five hundred, all in," she said. "Sign here."

Afterwards, he crossed the gallery and went down some steps. In a darkened room, he put the manila envelope on a table and switched on a chrome lamp. The light illuminated a cluttered work shop where varnishes, oils, books and easels fought for space. In a painting he was about to restore, the shadow of a city, Italian perhaps, could be made out under a layer of grime.

He sat down on a stool and looked at the envelope. It didn't weigh much. Less than the infant, he thought. He remembered holding the boy: the puce face wrinkled from the struggle of birth. Large, milky blue eyes. A tiny nose. A tiny mouth. A long time ago.

Richard picked up a Stanley knife from a row of tools. He opened the blade and slid it into a corner of the envelope. Then he stopped. He felt uncertain. I can't, he thought. I am too much of a coward to do this alone. And anyway, Katy should know.

*

The rain patted the soft top of the Triumph Spitfire as the vehicle headed west, down the King's Road, black smoke belting from the exhaust.

Richard peered through the windscreen. The wipers were on full but struggling to keep up with the rain. The car heater kept coughing like an old dragon trying to muster up fire. From the stereo, an erratic Jazz number, Flight to Jordan, added to the noise. While on the passenger seat, the manila envelope lay quietly next to a dog-eared exhibition catalogue.

Just one painting sold, Richard thought again, shaking his head and biting a nail. What can I do? Is it me? Or is it the market?

The Brownlowe gallery had been in the family for over half a century. Roland Brownlowe, Richard's grandfather, setting up the business in the 1950s. Then David, Richard's father, had taken over. Three years ago, Richard accepted the responsibility of running the gallery. But I don't have the Brownlowe touch, he thought, changing gear.

Richard parked the Triumph on Horder Road in Fulham. He got out of the vehicle and walked up to one of the terraced houses. The eggshell blue paint on the front door was a myriad of cracks. In the hall, pots, rollers and rags cluttered the floor. Why does Katy insist on doing reforms, he wondered, as he circumnavigated the mess.

On entering the living room, he found her smoking in an armchair in her dungarees. Her hair was uncombed, her brown eyes dull. The New Yorker was open on her lap. On a side table, a packet of Marlboro cigarettes, a Zipper lighter and an empty glass.

Katy placed the cigarette between her lips, took a long drag and exhaled. "You're back early," she said.

Richard wiped some sweat from his brow. Then he held up the manila envelope. "I've got something to show you," he replied.

2
Pandora's Box

It can't be true, Victor thought, as he poured himself a glass of water. It just can't be true. He drank quickly, putting the glass back down by the kitchen sink. It can't be true, he repeated, shaking his head. He stood there, staring at a bunch of dying margaritas in a vase. Dry petals had curled and scattered on the surface of the table.

He was tall with curly brown hair and blue eyes. Wearing a t shirt with the image of a monkey in a cage on the front, jeans and trainers. His head a whirl of confusion from a cocktail of alcoholic drinks and unsettling rumour. Lies, he thought, trying to smother the possibility.

Even so, he left the kitchen, went down the corridor and entered his father's study. It was warm and musty in here. The smell of cigar prevailed. He went over to the mahogany desk and switched on its lamp. The photograph of a younger Victor, posing on a ski slope, smiled back at him. But Victor didn't feel any better.

He sat on a leather chair and eased open the top drawer of the desk. Inside, there was a stapler, some letter-writing paper, envelopes and stamps. In the second drawer, he found bank statements and insurance documents. In the third drawer, electricity and phone bills. No proof though, he thought, leaning back. He watched a fly circle the light. In the background, half hidden in the darkness, a twisting bullfighter glared out from a painting on the wall. While in the garden, a cicada rubbed its wings.

*

He couldn't sleep so he lay in bed, thinking. He had been at a student bar off Recogidas when his cousin Lydia dropped the bomb. They were alone at that moment, Lydia's boyfriend, Miguel, getting the next round. "My mother mentioned it," she had said in a whisper. "How come you never said anything?"

"I never knew," he replied.

He had been quiet for the rest of the evening. Drinking that last beer quicker than the others, trying to keep a smile on his face. Then he had said goodnight and headed home. But he stopped off at another hang-out on the way, this one run down and almost empty, and ordered a Cuba libre at the bar.

The barman had hesitated, wondering how old the kid was, then he shrugged and poured rum into a glass full of ice. Victor had sat alone in the darkness of the bar. He drank slowly. The melting ice fractured. A lot of stuff, most of it dark, circling in his head.

Now, lying in bed at home, he remembered the shoe box. He had been told never to touch it. He climbed out of the bed and crossed the room. He was wearing a pair of boxer shorts and the t shirt, with the caged monkey on it.

His bare feet made no noise as he crept down the passage. He paused in the doorway of his parents' bedroom. His father was snoring on top of the king size bed. His mother was curled up in the foetal position, facing the other way. About half a metre separated the couple.

He walked over to a chest of drawers, knelt down and slowly eased open the bottom drawer. He could feel the soft wool of some jerseys. Then the shoe box beneath. He was about to lift it when his father muttered something. Victor remained still, head bowed, kneeling in the darkness. Leonardo said something else and turned over. Victor picked up the box and quietly closed the drawer. Then he crept out of the room.

He sat on the edge of his bed with the shoe box on his lap. At first, he just looked at it. And wondered if it should be opened. Then he slowly raised the lid releasing a musty smell of trapped paper. He picked up the top document. It was a birth certificate.

The certificate belonged to a Victor Roland Brownlowe. Born on 7/05/2000 in Edinburgh's Royal Maternity hospital. The name under *father* was: Richard Roland Brownlowe. The name under *mother* was: Katy Anne Shaw.

With trembling fingers, Victor put the document down and picked up the next one. It was an application for an adoption order. Also in English. Signed by Leonardo Garrido Valverde and Fiona Susan Newman.

Victor remained seated on the edge of the bed with the document in his hands. A numbing sensation crawled across his mind like a silent mist. Making his thoughts and body feel heavy. As if a nurse had administered a tranquillizer.

*

It was still dark outside when he put on some jeans and trainers. He pulled a black, thirty-five litre, Alpine rucksack from under his bed. He attached a roll mat to the bottom. Then he threw in a couple of jerseys, a pair of trousers and some shorts. He added another t shirt, pants and socks, not really thinking about it too much. He chucked in a few other possessions, including a penknife. Then he picked up his wallet and some change and slung the rucksack over his shoulder.

Before he left the room, he looked around: Pandora's box sat on the middle of the bed, the documents scattered around it, while his mobile phone occupied the corner of a shelf. I won't need that, he thought.

At the top of the stairs, he rested a hand on the wooden bannister and waited in the darkness. He wanted his father to appear and ask what he was doing. He wanted his mother to say that everything was all right. He wanted to be told they could sort it out together, as a family, like all the other problems that had been sorted out and subsequently forgotten. But his father didn't appear. Nor did his mother. So he went down the stairs and walked out of the house.

3
Separate Ways

"He's the spitting image of you," Katy cried, taking a gulp of whisky from a tumbler.

"But he's got your nose," Richard replied.

They were seated on the sofa in the sitting room. She, unkempt, still in her dungarees. He had taken off his jacket and tie. The manila envelope lay on the coffee table in front of them. So did a report, the whisky bottle and her cigarettes. And close-up photos of Victor and the parents, Leonardo and Fiona. Taken in quick succession, from a street corner.

She went slowly through these, her hands trembling. Tears rolling down her cheeks. Then she punched Richard. Hard.

"Why didn't you tell me?"

"I wanted it to be a surprise," he replied, rubbing his arm. She let out a small, high-pitched laugh.

"It's certainly a surprise!" She shook her head, unable to believe it. "It was so long ago Richard. Why now?"

"I just couldn't wait any more."

"But we gave him away. It's not our business."

"He's still our son." He said this softly.

She picked up the report and turned to the first page: Victor Garrido Newman. At least, they had kept the Christian name, she thought. Chosen to honour and remember her late grandfather. Victor lived at 37 Acacia Street. In Granada, Spain. In a different country. But he really was the boy. A copy of the birth certificate proved it. So did a form from the adoption agency.

"How did they get hold of this?" she asked.

"The detective agency has a huge web of connections."

She knew that was probably true. Anyway, it didn't matter. The memories were surfacing again. There was no way to stop them. Forgotten images. Buried feelings. Starving fish coming up to feed.

*

It's not right, Katy said to herself that afternoon, opening the door of a kitchen cupboard and reaching up. It's not our business any more. The cup she chose had a fading Superwoman flying across its face.

"Well, I'm not going anywhere," she muttered. Even so, she could not help thinking of 37 Acacia street, Granada. Wondering what it was like. Wondering what he was like. Wondering what *they* were like.

She poured strong coffee into the cup and added two teaspoons of brown sugar. Then she lit a cigarette. Toblerone came through the cat flap, shook the rain drops from his damp back and rubbed himself against her legs. With the cigarette between her lips, she stirred the coffee and carried the cup to a table.

She sat down in front of her lap top and moved her hair back, behind her ears. Then she stared at a list of contents on the screen.

Why did I enrol on this course? she thought. I hate the bloody subject. But she knew why she had chosen art history. To please Richard and the Brownlowe family.

She opened a document. It was about El Greco. The Greek, she thought, had lived in Spain too. She looked across the room at the manila envelope. It was sitting on a shelf. The images of her son came back to mind. Bloody Richard. How could he? She stubbed out the cigarette in a glass ashtray. Then she picked up the coffee cup. And observed its murky world.

Katy did some painting later: the wall by the stairs. Afterwards, she drank a glass of water. Then she left the house in her paint-splashed dungarees and old trainers. She walked across the park avoiding the huddle of mothers chatting by the swings. At the entrance to Tesco, she searched her pockets for a shopping list she had made. But it wasn't anywhere to be found.

It was with a vaguely unsettled feeling that she did the shop. And when, some thirty minutes later, she returned to Horder road, she unlocked the front door of the house, dropped her shopping bags and stumbled down the corridor, knocking over a paint pot.

In the kitchen, Toblerone was sitting on the window ledge, watching a veil of water cascade over the lip of the sink. Katy splashed through the pool below and turned off the tap.

She stood, breathing heavily, looking down at the water swilling around her ankles. A sweet wrapper was floating on the surface like a tiny boat on a lake. Then she saw the shopping list. Submerged. She bent down to pick it up. The ink on the soggy paper had run. Dissolving into different colours. Going their separate ways.

4
37 Acacia Street

"Yes, the flight was fine," Richard said in the stuffy heat of arrivals, Malaga airport. In front of him, the first suitcases had appeared on the carousel. "I even got some shut-eye. How's the decorating going? And the new assignment?"

He adjusted the phone against his ear, not really listening to Katy's reply. Guessing that she had made zero progress on both fronts. Then she said something about damp in the kitchen. Because of that flood, he thought. How could she have left the tap running?!

He wondered if Katy was going to be all right. She was on the antidepressants. And drinking too much. Despite her being dead against "the futile search for Victor" (her words), he had gone ahead anyway and booked his flight.

Now, in arrivals, a large woman leaned forward and grabbed a suitcase. So did a man whose pale arms were covered in tattoos. Further along, a group of teenagers were seated in a line like fledglings on a wire, sending text messages. A Samsonite suitcase appeared from the mouth of the carousel. Richard adjusted his phone. "Look," he said. "I'll ring back as soon as I get to the hotel. OK?"

When he had collected his luggage, he squeezed through the crowd, out of the airport building and into a wall of heat. Overhead, the afternoon sun blasted burning rays. The smell of dark tobacco hung in a heavy air and there was an aroma of strong coffee, reminding him of Italy.

He went to a taxi rank. A driver told him, in pigeon English, the price of a fare to Granada. "*Approvare*," Richard said without thinking. Then he remembered the Spanish word: "*Vale*."

It was cool inside the taxi. Richard leaned back and sighed. A sticker of the virgin mother gazed tearfully down from the ceiling. Pope Francis smiled from a calendar. Rosary beads dangled below the mirror.

The driver guided the vehicle out of the airport onto a ring road, dense with traffic. Later, the traffic thinned out and the road twisted upwards and away. Like a grapevine, Richard thought, freeing itself from the bedlam of Malaga. They entered a landscape of olive groves and parched fields. Some horses, heads bowed, stood in the shade of a tree in a paddock. The Osborne bull appeared, black and mighty against the skyline, showing off its balls.

At the top of a plateau, craggy ridges cut the landscape. Richard shifted uncomfortably in his seat. Why have I really come here, he asked himself. To look for my only son? Or to escape from Katy? And our dead-end marriage.

*

The four-star hotel Richard had booked, was an ugly block in the centre of town. It had been built in the early 70s and its open plan reception retained a certain fading grandeur: marble floors, fluted columns and wooden wall panels.

After checking in, he took the elevator to the sixth floor. His room had a double bed and an en-suite bathroom. He switched on the air-con and stood by the window. Outside, a grey Sierra Nevada loomed. He guessed the snows would probably come in November. When I am back in London, he thought. He picked up his mobile and phoned Katy again, as promised. But she didn't pick up so he left a message.

He had been given a map of the city and now he opened it up on the bed. It didn't take him long to find Acacia street. Part of him wanted to go and meet his son immediately. But he was tired after the journey. So he took off his shoes and lay down. Resting his head on the pillow, he stared upwards. At an old ceiling fan. Whose blades were still. Then he turned on his side and closed his eyes.

When Richard awoke, the city was bathing in the rusty glow of an evening sun. He took a shower, changed and left the hotel.

It was warm and still by the river Genil. The Granadino population was out in force: strolling or enjoying *tapas* on packed bar and restaurant terraces. At one of these, Richard ordered *una cerveza y un bocadillo de lomo* from an out-of-breath waitress.

Next to him, a group of thirty somethings were celebrating a birthday. Some teenagers whizzed by on mopeds. Two elegant young women walked past licking ice-creams perched on cones. Richard glanced at his watch. In the colder England he had left, he knew most people would already be inside.

After the drink and *tapas*, he continued along the river. He went past a school and then turned down another road. It didn't take him long to find number 37 Acacia street. It was a white house guarded by an imposing fence. And it appeared deserted: the window shutters were down, the driveway empty. A mountain bike with a flat front tyre was leaning against a wall. A couple of plastic chairs silently faced each other on the porch.

He put his hands in his pockets and wondered what to do. He tried Katy again. When she picked up, he told her that he had located the house. "But it doesn't look like anyone's there," he said.

"Perhaps they are on holiday," she replied.

"It's a nice pad," he added. "In a well-to-do part of town." Then he asked if she was going to Jerry Pakota's exhibition opening in Soho.

"I don't know," she said.

"Jean can't make it so try. You should get out a little."

After the call, Richard stood under a mimosa tree. The house remained empty; the shutters still down. The only movement was the flutter of leaves in a breeze.

5
Dog

Victor was squatting on a river bank, filling a water bottle. He was sunburnt and dirty, having slept rough for a few days. Beside him, rushes rustled in a breeze. A branch floated past. On the other side of the river, a wagtail was pacing up and down a muddy bank. He watched it as he drank. But he did not smile.

Why wasn't I told? he asked himself, still angry with his parents. And how come I never guessed? At the same time, he was wondering what sort of people would abandon an infant: Junkies? Down and outs? Teenage pregnancy? The latter had happened to a girl in the year above him at school.

He wondered if the biological parents even knew he existed. The bastard could be a criminal doing life. Or was he a millionaire oblivious of a biological son? He could be dead. And the woman? Was *she* alive? The possibilities swam in circles around his head.

After refilling the bottle, he put his rucksack on his back. And continued on the path by the river. It led him away, up a slope. At the top, the path joined a track which ran through an olive grove. The gnarled trees standing firm in the burning heat.

Outside a farm house, shards of broken glass glinted on the parched ground. A mastiff lay chained to a piece of machinery. Flies crawled around the animal's large, dopey eyes. The dog rose as Victor approached, rattling its chain. It pulled the chain tight, straining its huge body, and growled. Victor adjusted his rucksack and walked past, oblivious.

He followed the dusty track into some hills. They were covered by gorse and rosemary bushes and clusters of *esparto* grass. Grasshoppers scattered before him on the track, their wings flashing pink or blue. Small lizards scurried away.

A little black dog appeared from out of nowhere, wagging its tail. After dipping its head, it crawled towards him in subservience. Then it rolled over and lay on its back, with its dusty paws in the air. Victor reached down and tickled its blotchy, pink stomach.

"Where's your owner?" he asked looking around, squinting. But there was no one in sight.

He continued on and the dog went beside him. He could feel the bright sun burn his nose and crack his lips. His trainers rubbed against his ankles and formed blisters. He drank the water. Sometimes he cupped his hand and gave some to the dog. Eventually, the last drops sunk into the pores of his tongue like rain on a dry river bed.

He stood on the track and the dog stood in his shadow. It was silent. He was far away from the city now. There was no breeze. High above, two griffon vultures circled in the sky.

As the sun was setting, he entered a ruin on the side of a hill. Its roof had caved in long ago and the walls were crumbling away.

He took out his roll mat and sleeping bag. He placed them by the remains of a wall. Then he lay down and rested his head on a folded jersey.

He lay there staring up at the streaks of red in the sky. Listening to the humming of the cicadas. The dog curled up beside him. He began shivering yet his body was burning. Part of him wanted to return home but another part was too proud. The stars came out one by one. He wanted to cry but no tears came.

6
The Exhibition

Katy had told Richard through tears, one spring afternoon in a park in Edinburgh. And watched the blood slowly drain from his face. Afterwards, they went to a pub. They sat in a corner in silence. Not like parents-to-be, celebrating new life, more like mourners following the news of a death.

"My parents will freak," Richard had eventually said.

"Mine too," Katy replied.

Over the following week, they went through the options: keep the child, foster care, even abortion. In the end, they decided to give the baby away for adoption. It seemed the easiest option, the least painful road to take. When we should have just kept him, Katy thought.

She used to think their foolishness could be understood from a social context. Education was first. Followed by a job. Then family. In that order. The words 'Earn Money and Enjoy Success!' had once flashed across an illuminated screen in her mind. Children weren't part of that equation.

Part of her believed that the child would not be given away. That she and Richard would come to their senses. Even when they were talking to a counsellor. Even when they had signed the papers. Even when she had broken water. Even when she had given birth. Even when the baby was gone.

"So where is your husband?" Tina, a blonde, asked, breaking Katy's reverie, and handing her a glass of champagne. They were at Jerry Pakota's exhibition opening in Notting Hill. Katy had taken Richard's advice and got out of the house. She was wearing a plain dress and a pair of sandals unlike Tina whose shiny dress, Gucci shades and high heels made her look like a film star.

"Granada," Katy replied. "He's gone to Granada."

"Isn't that the Caribbean love?"

Katy shook her head. "Not Grenada. Granada, Spain. It's north of Malaga."

Tina lowered the Gucci shades. "Well, why aren't you with him doll?" she asked.

Katy shrugged and took a sip of champagne.

"We just dig the Costa, don't we Shiva?" Tina then said to a dog in her arms. The dog just stared back. "Oh, and Jerry comes too."

Katy laughed and looked to the centre of the room where Jerry stood surrounded by male admirers. A gold medallion winked between the open buttons of his Lycra shirt. In front of them, a lurid painting hung on the wall. Who would buy such a monstrosity? Katy wondered. But it was impossible to guess: the number of suspects in the crowded room was large.

"Have you seen his Neon Horse?" Tina asked.

"Sounds dangerous," Katy replied, shaking her head.

Now it was Tina's turn to laugh. "There's a copy over there. It's a piece of shit if you ask me but it's worth two million so it pays the bills. The original is currently galloping round the lobby of the Rosewood hotel in Abu Dhabi."

Katy shook her head in disbelief. Then she spotted something fizzing away in the base of her glass. "What is that?" she asked.

"Just a little pick-me-up love." Tina replied. "Looks like you could do with a lift."

*

An hour later, Katy was on the pavement outside a nightclub. Feeling pretty good. In fact, she hadn't felt better. Not for a long time. Since when? she wondered. Since the parties she had gone to when she had moved back down south after Edinburgh, an unemployed graduate and childless mother.

Yet the passing of time did not seem to matter for now. Her mainly solitary, unhappy life was temporarily forgotten. So was her hand bag with her credit card, money and cigarettes. They were lying on the back seat of a limousine which had just pulled away.

Tina Pakota was beckoning the group of exhibition-goers towards the nightclub entrance. Shiva, the dog, still under one of her arms. Katy went with them. While the others chatted, she was quiet. There was something childlike in her manner, in the way she looked around. She felt safe surrounded by these people and their noise.

In a dimly-lit foyer, a female bouncer was taking tickets. This huge woman had rings in her eyebrows and little scars on her cheeks. A tattoo of a serpent coiled around her neck.

"Let us through Baroness," Tina said. "This lot are with me."

"As you wish," the woman replied, standing aside.

The group made their way down a long corridor. It was studded with portholes taken from a cruise ship which had run aground in the 1970s. Katy peered through a window, touching the glass with her fingers. A ray glided past. Then a shoal of silver fish. Below, anemones and star fish clung to rocks and coral. There were sponges too.

It's like being a child again, she thought. Then, peering into the depths of the blue void, she glimpsed a darker shape. "Is that a shark?" she wondered, turning but the others had moved on. Katy looked again. All she could see now was her own distorted reflection in the glass. She frowned. Then she walked on, drawn by a mesmerising beat of drums.

7
One Step Closer

Despite the fact it had just gone eight, bright sunlight penetrated the hotel room. Richard, leaning over the sink in the bathroom, splashed water on his face. Then he put on a t shirt, shorts and trainers.

He left the room and took the elevator down to a restaurant where he had coffee and toast. Afterwards, he exited the hotel and walked along the river Genil. Only a narrow film of water ran across its concrete bed. Giving it the status of a stream, he thought. He passed a secondary school. And wondered if Victor attended it. Perhaps, I will find out today, he thought.

On Acacia street, the shutters of number 37 were up. A Volvo estate was parked in the driveway. A canvas bag sat beside the plastic chairs on the porch. So this is it, Richard thought. But he didn't move to ring the bell. He just stood in the street under the mimosa tree, hands in his pockets, and waited.

Fifteen minutes later, Richard was sitting in a quiet café a little further down Acacia street. There was a *café solo* in front of him. The two customers on the next door table were chatting about the metro.

Richard kept looking through the window of the café. Why didn't I ring the bell? he asked himself. Because you're frightened!

Admit it. You're frightened of what you might discover. Of who you might find. And of what might happen.

Now he could see two people coming out of the house. They were walking down the street. Towards the café. It was Leonardo and Fiona, Victor's parents. Leonardo tanned, his hair greased back, wearing a white shirt and pressed chinos. Fiona, slightly sunburned, in a summer dress.

From a distance, they looked like a model European couple. But as they neared, Richard saw there was distance between them. Like they had just had an argument. After they had passed, he paid the waiter and left the café. He walked up to the house. Victor will be there, he thought. But the shutters were down again.

It took him ten minutes to locate Leonardo and Fiona again. He followed them down a busy road called Manuel de Góngora. They turned down a side street and walked through a small park, dotted with orange trees. Over the far side of the park, there was a line of businesses. Leonardo opened the shutter of one of these. The sign above it read: Newman School of English.

When Leonardo and Fiona had gone inside, Richard approached warily; like a tomcat that has strayed into foreign territory. He read the information in the window: a range of Cambridge English courses on offer for all ages and levels. Including B1 and B2 courses. Whatever they are, he thought. And:

Native Teacher Wanted
No experience Necessary

Richard stared at the advert. Then he took a deep breath, pushed the door open and walked inside. He hadn't noticed the poster of a missing boy on a board further along the school's façade.

8
The Café with No Name

Victor was walking down a track towards a village nestled in a valley. It was noon and the sun was high. A fine layer of dust covered his hair, his sunburnt face and his clothes. His left trouser leg was torn. It had got snagged on barbed wire while he had tried to climb through a fence. The dog was still with him but as they neared the first houses, it slunk away. So that made Victor think.

Victor walked silently into the village. Many of the houses looked abandoned: their windows smashed, their roofs in disrepair. In a street, a mule had been tied to a ring on a wall. Olive branches nestled in baskets on each side of its back. It stood with head bowed, flicking its tail from side to side. But the flies smothering its eyes remained.

In the centre of the village, there was a square with an old church on one side. Victor went over to the fountain in the middle of the square. Two old men watched from a bench under the shade of an orange tree. They were wearing trilby hats, thin cotton shirts, slacks and *esparto* shoes. They watched Victor cup his hands below a trickle of water and drink. Afterwards, he washed his face. Then he looked around. On another side of the square, there was a café. It didn't have a name.

There were only two other people inside the café with no name. One was scrubbing a greasy pan in the kitchen and the other was behind the bar, drying glasses. They were the Vega Brothers. Juan Vega, drying the glasses behind the bar, was a big guy. He weighed 95 kilos and had a large mole on his neck. Sergio Vega, who was in the kitchen, was five ten and wirier but no less mean looking. Both men had served time in Albolote prison and correctional facility.

Juan Vega studied Victor as he put down his rucksack by an empty table and walk over to the bar. From a wall, the stuffed head of a male ibex, its horns long and curved, appeared to watch the stranger too.

When Victor reached the bar, he greeted Juan Vega.

"¿Que quieres?" Juan Vega asked. His voice was rough and his tone was unwelcoming.

"Something to eat," Victor replied.

Juan Vega passed over a grease-stained menu.

Victor scanned it. He ordered a steak, chips and a salad.

"How do you want the steak?"

"Medium rare," Victor said.

"And to drink?"

"A Coke with ice."

When the meal came, Victor dug in. The steak was tough and the chips tasted like the rancid oil they had been cooked in, but he ate the food because he was ravenous. And he drunk the Coke too although it was warm.

It was only afterwards, when he was wondering if he could afford a dessert, that Victor patted his trouser pocket and realised his wallet was missing. He sat there trying to work out where he had put it. It must be in my rucksack, he thought. So he checked the pockets. But the wallet was not in the rucksack.

While he sat wondering what to do, Juan Vega came over and asked if he wanted anything else. "*Un flan,*" Victor said. Juan nodded and went to tell his brother. Victor went to the toilet. He stood in the toilet and urinated and his heart was beginning to race. When he came out of the toilet, he could hear the men talking in the kitchen. So he picked up his rucksack and walked silently out of the café.

9
High

On the tightly packed dance floor of the nightclub, Katy punched a balloon in the air. While strobe lights span, slowing time. Globules of sweat rolled down her shiny face. Her breasts pressed against the material of her dress. While her heart thumped to the relentless beat of electronic music, her mind span with ideas. She twirled and cheered. Anything is possible, she thought, I can do anything!

"Are you all right?" Tina shouted, grabbing her hand and pulling her to the side.

"Am I all right?" Katy shouted back. "I haven't felt like this for years!"

Tina laughed. "If you say so. But I think you need to calm down."

Katy let Tina guide her off the dance floor and up a staircase. At the top of this, there was a chill-out bar. Soft, blue light coloured the walls. The sound of waves could be heard breaking on a pebble beach. Sea stones, Katy thought. They ordered cocktails: Katy's was a Gin Sling while Tina chose a Pina Colada.

They carried the drinks over to a couple of vacant beanbags. Katy unfastened her sandals. "That's better," she said sitting down and wiggling her toes. She looked up and gazed at a cartoon dog, running across a screen. "Although I could really do with a fag." Then she sighed, lifted the cocktail and felt the cool liquid slide down her throat.

"Do you know why my husband has gone to Granada?" Katy asked Tina a few moments later.

"I haven't a clue love," Tina replied.

Katy leaned forward. "Can you keep a secret?"

Tina shook her head. "Not usually."

"Well, try please."

*

"So Richard's quest is futile," Katy concluded half an hour later, wiping away some tears. "No good will come of it. We can't just go and dig the past up when the whim takes us. We shouldn't interfere. It's up to our son to come to us, isn't it?"

"But what if he doesn't?" Tina replied. "Don't you want to know what he's like?"

"That's what Richard said.".

"Well, I can see his point of view."

Katy sighed. "Our marriage is a farce," she concluded. "If you hadn't already worked it out."

"So is mine," Tina whispered. "Just the other day, I came home to find Jerry in bed with a close friend of his."

Katy looked horrified. "What did you do?"

"I threw them and the bed out."

Katy laughed. Then she frowned

"But what are you going to do now?"

"Nothing. We're staying together."

"Why?"

Tina shrugged. "He pays for my lifestyle love. He lets me do what I want."

They are like plates, Katy thought later, in the ladies room, studying the huge pupils of her brown eyes in a mirror. It was four in the morning. She was standing next to Tina who was putting on eye-liner and humming. Shiva, the chihuahua, was sitting on the edge of the sink. The dog seemed to be studying Katy, its pink tongue poking through its teeth.

"Need another pick-me-up doll?" Tina asked taking a small, silver box out of her handbag. She clicked it open revealing half a dozen white pills nestled on a bed of velvet.

"I think that would be a bad idea," Katy replied. "I have to leave soon."

"But the party's still going."

"Not for me, it isn't. And you said I really need to get in touch with myself."

"Well, these will help. You might as well enjoy yourself while you can. *Carpe diem* and all that, love."

Katy looked at Tina; thinking about it, wanting to regain that high. "How many have you had?"

"Just five," Tina said. She held up another between her fingers. Then she popped it in her mouth and drank some champagne. "That's number six."

Katy shook her head and laughed. "You're nuts."

She was aware that she was letting this woman influence her. It was a pattern of behaviour she was familiar with. As a child, she had followed her big sister, Deborah, around and copied her every move.

Later, she had sought friends who were bolder and brighter than her. Girls who liked the limelight and who took control.

Girls who made decisions under whose supervision she could follow safely. Life with Richard mirrored that pattern, she thought. She just did what she was told, obeying him most of the time.

Now, here she was, at thirty four, in a night club about to pop a pill. Why? Because Tina, the woman who had spiked her champagne earlier, had taken six.

10
The NSE

Richard was sitting in an office, facing Fiona Newman across an oval shaped desk. She looks exhausted, he thought, noticing dark shadows under her eyes, like she doesn't sleep well at night. When he had entered the school, she had cried out. As if I was a ghost who had just walked through a wall, he thought.

He hadn't said that he was Victor's biological father. Instead he had asked about the teaching vacancy, advertised outside the school Fiona and Leonardo ran.

When Fiona turned to her computer screen, Richard looked around the room: at a framed teaching diploma that was hanging next to a linguistics degree, at text books on a bookcase, at a metallic blue filing cabinet and a Rank Xerox photocopier.

The telephone rang. Instead of picking up, Fiona glanced through a window, obscured by the slats of a lowered blind, into reception. Leonardo appeared and answered, LED light shining down onto his slick, black hair. Richard had shaken his hand earlier and looked into cold eyes.

"What did you say your surname was?" Fiona asked.

"Brown," he lied, thinking it was close enough.

"Don't you have any teaching experience at all?"

"I taught English to a couple of kids in Rome on my Erasmus year," he replied.

"Rome is a great city," Fiona said and for a moment her eyes shone. "What part did you live in?"

"Trastevere. You've visited?"

"We celebrated our tenth anniversary there. And stayed in this incredible hotel near the Colosseum." She looked back to reception where Leonardo was now sitting. "But that all seems long ago." She shrugged as if dismissing the thought. "Any other experience apart from teaching those kids?"

"Nothing," Richard.

"But you speak Italian?"

"Right. I've got a joint honours degree in Italian and History of Art. And I took Spanish A level as well."

"Good. Knowledge of a foreign language is essential for this teaching position." Fiona leaned back appearing to relax. "I haven't asked what you do."

"I am an art dealer."

"Oh?" Fiona replied, raising an eyebrow. "We don't get many art dealers in here."

"I don't suppose you do."

"So why teaching?"

*

"There are two hundred and twelve students enrolled," Fiona told Richard some time later while they went up a flight of stairs to the first floor. "Adults, teens and kids. The majority of students come in the afternoon but some of the adults attend morning classes."

At the top of the stairs, they made their way down a corridor. In a classroom, she pointed out an electronic whiteboard, laptop and air con. "It's state-of-the-art equipment," she said.

Then they went to the staff room. There was a table littered with texts books and other teaching materials, a book shelf, a computer, a photocopier and a small kitchen. "We use a communicative approach," she explained picking up a resource book. "Students role play, have discussions, solve problems and things like that. All in English, of course."

"Sounds different from the language classes at my old school," Richard said. "We just went through the conjugation of verbs. Mr. Small was the head of department but no one could understand what he said. Neither in French nor Spanish nor English."

"We had an old crone called Miss Barnes," Fiona said. "She spent her life shouting at us. I think she was a bit nuts."

*

Afterwards, Richard walked to the centre of town. He passed the church of Our Lady of Sorrows. Outside the church, a couple of Romanian women, with gold in their teeth and shawls draped over their shoulders, were on their knees, begging. Victor cursed himself. Not because of the presence of the beggars or the fact he had no change on him, but because he wished he had just told Fiona and Leonardo who he was.

At least Victor is being brought up by decent folks, he thought. Well, Fiona's nice. Attractive too. He smiled because Fiona appeared to have been seriously considering him as an applicant. One that could be trained up. He tried to imagine himself standing in front of a class but couldn't. I was a terrible teacher in Rome, he thought.

He went past a fountain called La Fuente de las Batallas. and through Puerta Real, a congested zone where vehicles, pedestrians and buildings fought for space. Then down a couple of streets to the cathedral. He didn't enter though. He admired the exterior with its decorative stonework. Diego de Siloé had worked on the building, he knew. Then Alonso Cano.

Afterwards, he went to the law faculty. But it was closed. There was a small art gallery near by. And a second hand book store. In the latter, he bought a simplified version of Don Quijote de la Mancha for three euros. He sat and tried to read it in a square in the shade of a fir tree. There were orange and lemon trees. And an Aleppo pine too.

It was quiet here. A tramp was curled up on a bench not far away. His head resting on a leather bag. There was a hunk of bread on the floor below the tramp. Some sparrows landed and began pecking at the scattered crumbs.

11
On the Run

Victor sprinted through the village, his heart beating fast. He kept looking over his shoulder, any moment expecting to hear shouts and running feet. When he had passed the last house, he slowed for a moment to get his breath back and adjust the rucksack on his back. Then he ran on, down a dirt track and into a valley.

After a while, he slowed again and walked. His heartbeat became regular. The tension in his neck subsided. There was only the noise of his feet on the track and the cicadas. A couple of buntings flitted silently ahead of him. At the bottom of a valley, a horse was grazing beside a bright green field of maize.

The little, black dog reappeared. It wagged its tail and lay on its back with its dusty paws in the air. Victor reached down and tickled its stomach. Then the dog rolled over and ran off, just in front of him. As he followed the dog down the track, he felt better. I must be losing my mind though, doing a thing like that, he thought. I should go back home. Quit while I'm ahead.

After a kilometre, he came to a fork in the track. There was a signpost but it had fallen to the ground. It was littered with bullet holes. Victor chose a narrow path to the left which snaked down the bare hillside. The dog followed.

On the track above, a vehicle appeared. It was a Jeep, billowing dust. When it slowed to a stop, the Vega brothers, the owners of the café Victor had run from, got out. Juan Vega took a hunting rifle from a rack. It was a bolt action Mossberg. He loaded it, knelt down and rested the barrel on a rock. Closing an eye, he looked down the hillside, through the telescopic sight. Sergio stood beside his brother. He was holding a pair of binoculars.

When a puff of dust jumped on the path, a couple of metres ahead of Victor, Victor jumped too. Then the gun shot report echoed off the hillside. Another shot was fired. The second shot smacked into the ground at Victor's feet. The next bullet hit the dog on the shoulder. It span around, yelping. Victor grabbed the dog and it bit him on the hand but he held onto it and dived forward.

They slid down the hillside. They slid through grit, gorse, rosemary and *esparto* grass until they hit the bottom of a gulley. Victor rose coughing, took off his rucksack and lowered it to the ground. He was covered in dust. The dust was in his hair and up his nose and in his mouth. Blood ran from a cut next to his right eye. He lay flat against the side of the hill with the dog in his arms. His hand pounded where the dog had bitten him. The dog whimpered. He stroked it. Then it stretched out a paw, shuddered and died.

Victor ran for cover with the dog still in his arms. A bullet whistled overhead and tore into the undergrowth. Another shot rang out. He stood in the safety of the trees by the river, catching his breath. Then he climbed down the bank and into the water.

It came up to his knees. He lowered the dog. And watched as it floated down stream. "Thanks for taking that bullet and saving my life," he whispered.

Then he turned and waded upstream. He waded a while. Eventually, he climbed up the far bank and crawled under a fallen tree.

He lay there, trying to keep his breathing steady. He could smell mud and damp leaves. He could feel a burning sensation where the dog had bitten his hand. A mosquito whined in his ear. A line of ants filed past his face. He wondered if he would ever see his parents again.

12
Cracking Up

Katy was lying on the dance floor surrounded by people. She had just vomited. But the music still thumped and the strobe lights span. Someone helped her up. "Are you all right?" another person asked. She nodded, wiping some slime from her mouth with the back of her hand. Then she wobbled unsteadily away.

Time to go home, she thought, when she had made it to the edge of the dance floor. Tina wasn't around so she trod bare foot down the dimly lit passage to the exit. Barely noticing a barracuda gliding silently by a port hole window. In the ticket office, Baroness, the bouncer, sat hunched over her mobile phone. She only looked up when Katy had gone through the door.

Katy walked along a pavement shrouded by a grey and overcast dawn. She couldn't hear its chorus, only a loud ringing in her ears. Occasionally, a chip of gravel would dig into the soles of her bare feet. On either side of the road, old warehouses loomed. They were grey and sinister with broken windows and crumbling walls, survivors of London's past.

It began spitting so Mascara slowly dribbled down her face. A car drove past. A passenger, wearing a leather jacket, leaned out of the window and whistled. Further on, she passed someone curled up, asleep in a cardboard box. A truck rumbled past. She walked on. She began to cry and then to laugh hysterically.

Something had cracked in her mind. Pieces were falling. Scattering like jagged leaves. She could feel the chemicals circulating. Whizzing around her brain. Much too fast, she thought. Like psychedelic motorbikes speeding round a circuit. In the wrong direction.

Now she stopped and leaned against a wall. Then she collapsed. She lay with a cheek pressed on the cold pavement. She could see a car parked but it was the wrong way up. She could make out a building. On its side. She could feel her heart beating. But it seemed far away. Alien. Something that didn't belong to her.

She shivered. She thought of Richard and wondered where he was. She thought of her parents. She thought of a room at the top of a house. She heard someone playing a piano.

13
Perdido

Richard was sitting at the end of an empty pew in a Baroque church. The place oozed incense and melancholy. There was marble and gold. Spiral columns. Virgins and saints, in various states of agony, occupied obscure niches and alcoves. And the faces of angels could be made out gazing down from huge paintings. They are falling from the sky, Richard thought.

He left the church and walked down a cobbled street towards the hotel. He passed a police station, then a Super Sol supermarket. A wall was plastered in posters. One was flapping in a breeze. He stared at the blown-up image of a familiar, fading face.

¿Has visto a este hombre?
Victor Garrido Newman
Esta perdido
desde el 29 de Agosto cuando
salió de su casa en Granada.
Si has visto a Victor o sabes
dónde esta, por favor llámenos.
Su familia y amigos están muy preocupados.
Tel 958 67 8990. Móvil: 661 245078.

Have you seen Victor Garrido Newman?
He's missing.
Since 29th August when he left home in Granada.
If you have seen Victor or know
where he is, please call us.
His family and friends are very worried.
Tel 958 67 8990. Movil: 661 245078.

Richard looked at the date again. It was the same day the courier had delivered the manila envelope to the Brownlowe gallery.

*

Back in the hotel, Richard wondered what to do. Victor was missing. So now what? His mobile rang. It was Fiona. "The job's yours if you want it," she told him. Then she went through some details: the responsibilities of an English language teacher, training, hours, school policy. "How does that sound?" she concluded.

"Sounds great," he replied.

"Can you come in tomorrow to sign the contract?"

"Sure," he replied.

After the call, he threw the mobile on the bed. Then he opened the mini fridge and grabbed a 5 cl bottle of whisky.

What game are you playing? he thought unscrewing the cap and taking a swig. The whisky burned the back of his throat and ran wild in his stomach.

The mobile rang again. He expected to see Fiona's name on the screen again. But it was his father.

"Hello Dad," he said warily.

"When are you coming back to London?" the older man replied, diving straight in.

"I don't know."

"What do you mean by that."

Richard said: "I might extend my holiday a little."

"How long for?"

"A week or two."

"Why?"

"I need to think."

"Can't you think here?"

"I need a break Dad."

"What about the gallery?"

"Jean is more than capable."

"Is she?"

"She knows the ropes."

There was a pause in the exchange. Richard imagined his father trying to work out what was going on and when the older man spoke again, his voice was more careful:

"What about Katy? Why isn't she with you?"

"She preferred to stay in London," Richard said. Then he quickly ended the call before any more questions could be asked.

Afterwards, he turned off the mobile phone, polished off the bottle of whisky and grabbed another from the mini fridge. All the time, he pictured his father relaying the information to his mother. Mum will start worrying, he thought. He drank the second bottle sitting on the edge of the bed. He felt calmer about the decision to stay on. At least, I can get to the bottom of this, he thought, find out exactly what is going on and where the hell Victor has got to.

14
Shall We Kill Him?

Victor was lying on damp leaves under the branches of a fallen tree. Blood, from the cut by his eye, had congealed. The hand, which the dog had bitten, was swollen. It throbbed. A mosquito inserted its proboscis into the skin on his ankle but he didn't move.

He could make out a figure coming towards him. It was Juan Vega, the owner of The Café With No Name. Creeping along the river bank. Coming closer. Carrying a rifle.

When Juan Vega was a couple of feet away, he stopped and lowered the rifle to the ground. He was sweaty and out of breath. After recovering, he took out a packet of Ducados. He put a cigarette between his lips and lit up. "I know you're in there," he said looking directly at where Victor was lying. "So come on out. I'll give you ten seconds." Yet there was no hurry in his speech.

By the time Sergio Vega crossed the river, Victor was on his feet. "Where was the *cabron*, Juan?" Sergio asked, wiping sweat from his forehead.

Vega elder pointed the rifle at the fallen tree. "Hiding under there."

Sergio spat. "Why did you leave us in such a hurry, kid?"

“Why was the dog shot?” Victor replied.

Sergio stepped up and punched Victor in the stomach. Victor doubled over. Sergio hit him again. Victor fell to the ground. “Fucking thief,” he added, kicking Victor.

Afterwards, he checked Victor’s pockets. “Where is your wallet?” he said. Victor grunted. Sergio kicked Victor another time. “Shall we kill him?” he asked his brother. Juan shook his head. “He’s not worth it.”

Sergio nodded. Then he stepped on Victor’s bloated hand, pressing the heel of his left boot down and twisting. There was a crunching sound. Victor cried out.

A short time later, the men walked away leaving Victor moaning on the ground. His face was puffed up, his ribs felt like they were fractured and his hand ached and burned like hell. He wanted to rise, hobble down to the river and dip the throbbing hand into the water to cool it down. But he didn’t have the strength to get up. So he just lay there. It had occurred to him that the dog was rabid. He didn’t care if he became infected. Part of him wanted to die anyway.

15
Footsteps

A police car came down the street and slowed to a stop alongside a woman in her thirties. The woman was sitting on the pavement with her knees up and her back against a wall. She was shaking. Two officers got out of the vehicle. One, female, grabbed a blanket from the back seat.

"What's your name, love?" she asked while she wrapped the blanket round the woman's shoulders.

The woman didn't reply.

The policewoman took out a light and shone it in the woman's eyes. "Have you taken anything tonight love?"

There was no response. Then the officer studied the woman's bloody bare feet. "Are you homeless?"

The woman shook her head.

"Where do you live?"

"Fulham," the woman whispered.

"What are you doing all the way out here?" the man asked.

The woman didn't reply.

"What's your name?" the female officer repeated.

The woman was silent.

"Look, we can take you to the station if you prefer and ask you there."

"Katy," the woman said. Her voice sounded far away.

The officers helped Katy up and she was guided to the car. The policewoman sat beside her in the back. The man got in the front and spoke into the radio. Then he started the engine and the car moved off.

"If you tell me what happened, we'll take you home," the woman asked.

"I don't know. I was in a nightclub. Then I ended up walking home and lost my way."

"And your shoes by the looks of things. What happened to them?"

"I don't know."

"Did you take anything last night Katy?"

She nodded.

"What?"

"I don't know."

"Did you buy it?"

She shook her head. "My drink was spiked."

"Who by?"

"A woman."

"A friend of yours?"

Katy shook her head. "We just got talking." Katy started shaking again. "I don't know how I ended up like this," she said. Then she closed her eyes. The man looked at the woman in the rear-view mirror. The radio crackled and the voices of other patrols could be heard.

*

When they arrived at the house, the policewoman accompanied Katy to the door. Katy found a spare key under a plant pot and unlocked the front door.

"Anyone else inside?" the woman asked.

Katy shook her head.

The woman gave Katy a leaflet. "You can ring this number if you need any help," she said. "In any case, someone will come round tomorrow to check up on you."

"I'll be OK," Katy said.

"It's procedure," the woman replied.

Katy stood by the door as the woman got back in the car. She watched the car move away. Then she went inside. In the kitchen, she made a cup of tea. The smell of damp lingered. Toblerone was out. The music from the club still pounded in her head.

She went upstairs with her tea and ran the bath. She unbuttoned her dress and let it fall to the floor. Then she took off her bra and pants and sat down on the wooden toilet seat. She sat and watched the steam rise from the hot water.

She climbed into the bath and lay submerged, with her head above the water's surface, propped against the back of the bath. Sweat and condensation glistened on her face. The music pounded. The people she had met and seen appeared and reappeared in her mind's eye. Images began to speed up. They rushed by, like fast-moving trains, one after another.

Going back. Looking down on herself. Unhappy. Childless. Depressed. Lonely. When had it all started to go wrong? She searched for a moment in time. And went back to Edinburgh, back to her pregnancy. Her hands resting on her swollen belly. Feeling the baby kick. Breaking water. Being helped by Richard down some wooden stairs, onto an icy street and into a freezing car. Pink furry dice swinging from the rear-view mirror on the way to the hospital. Lying on a bed. Being wheeled down a corridor. Contractions. Screaming.

She lay, staring upwards, listening to her heart thumping against her chest. Her hair fanned out in the water. Sweat oozing from the pores in her skin. She thought she heard a key turning in the front door. Has Richard returned? she wondered. Now footsteps were slowly coming up the stairs. She tried to get up. But she couldn't move. She tried to scream. But her voice made no sound.

AUTUMN

1
Fiona

Sunshine filtered through the sitting room window of a third floor flat. It dappled the floor and made a pattern on the worn sofa where Richard was settled, surrounded by text books. He was marking homework while listening to Radio 4 on his lap top.

Richard had completed his training at the NSE. Finding the week long, in-house course and its various modules challenging. Then he had been assigned a series of afternoon classes. He found the work rewarding on the whole. A breath of fresh air, he thought. At least for now. However, it seemed to him that financially, language teaching was a limited profession.

Victor was still missing. Richard had hired a Granada based detective agency to look for the boy but they had been ineffectual (and expensive). In fact, Richard had only learned two things through the agency: 1) Victor was unhappy at home and unsettled at high school. 2) He had only recently discovered he was adopted.

Katy was another worry. Since Richard had told her he was staying in Granada, she wouldn't speak to him.

Richard got up and left the room. He walked down the corridor to the kitchen where he poured himself a glass of water. He stood, holding the glass and looked through the kitchen window onto the terrace. I am lucky, he thought. This place is a far cry from the string of holes I saw back in the summer: one had mould running up the walls I recall, in another cats roamed wild and the third place stank of urine.

After seeing those flats, he had wandered the boiling streets of Granada disgruntled. Finding refuge from the heat in a hairdressers where he had told a tubby barber (whose eyes appeared to pop out of the thick lenses of his glasses) about his dilemma.

"There's a vacant flat in the block where I live," the man had said. "My mother-in-law owns it. In fact, she owns the whole building."

So he had been shown around and the following day, he moved in.

After changing and picking up his wallet, Richard locked the flat and descended the stone stairs. On the floor below, a face peered through a crack in a door. This was Pilar, the wife of Gonzalo, the hairdresser, and was all Richard usually saw of the woman. Unless they happened to pass each other on the street or stairs. If this happened, she would rush by him, eyes down.

The door quickly closed. Richard continued to the bottom of the stairs. Crossing the hall whose floor tiles had images of stars, suns and moons. Outside, it was pleasantly warm and bright. He walked down the street to a square. Pausing at an old bench to retie a shoe lace.

Nearby, a pigeon was squatting on the head of a statue. It was of Mariana Piñeda and the square was named after her. Mariana

Piñeda had been a rebel and a heroine. She was executed after helping her cousin, a liberal, escape from prison. A flag was discovered at her house with the slogan 'Equality, Freedom and Law' embroidered on it. Dangerous words in an absolute kingdom.

Richard crossed the square and walked under the arches of Ángel Ganivet. Ganivet had been a writer, Richard knew.

One that was concerned with the spiritual condition of his country. He had been able to speak five languages but suffered a progressive disease. Then he drowned himself in the Daugava river in Riga, Latvia. 'Another victim of love's cruel cup,' Richard thought, shaking his head.

On Mesones, he checked out the clothes shops; buying two shirts, a pair of jeans, a jersey and a jacket. It was as he left the last shop, that he bumped into Fiona. Victor's mother was wearing shades and a leather coat.

"I see you've been spending your wages," she said looking down at the bags he now carried.

"I have indeed," Richard replied. "The evenings are getting colder now."

"In November, the temperature really drops."

"So I hear."

Like Richard, Fiona had finished her morning tasks and had some free time, so they decided to go for a coffee in Bib-Rambla square.

They entered the square and sat down at a table outside a restaurant. Fiona took out a packet of cigarettes and lit up. Richard watched her. And he wondered why he was attracted to women who smoked. "This is so different from the UK," he said.

Fiona exhaled and nodded. "I was brought up in Slough. Not much café culture then."

Richard smiled and added. "Or now, I imagine."

A group of Japanese appeared and began snapping away at the fountain of Neptune. Then, like a regiment called to order, the Japs got into single file and marched off.

Fiona balanced the burning cigarette on the edge of an ashtray. "So how's your wife?" she asked. "Is she going to come over soon?"

Richard shook his head. "She's depressed. Not well enough to travel."

"That's a pity."

He shrugged. "It's probably for the better."

"What do you mean?"

"It's difficult to explain."

"Try me."

"Well, she's changed. I sometimes think she's not the same woman I married."

Fiona leaned forward. "I understand. Look at Leonardo! When we met, he was a carefree student who could laugh until dawn. Now he's become so cold and serious, I wonder where that student went."

An image of Leonardo pacing the corridors of the school came to Richard's mind. He thought of Victor. After hesitating, he asked: "Is that why your son left home?"

Fiona looked at Richard. "Partly, I think."

"And the other part?"

"It's a long story." She picked up the cigarette, sliding it between two fingers, but kept her eyes on Richard. "Every time I go home, I expect Victor to be standing outside the gate. When he isn't, my heart sinks. But what can we do? He is an adult in the eyes of the law. There is no way to help him. Except wait for his return."

2
The Gorge

Victor was walking along a mule path in a valley. His hair was longer and curlier and his cheeks were sunken. He was all skin and bones. His t shirt was baggy and his trousers were loose around the waist. His trainers were falling apart, the soles worn out. But his eyes were bright. Six weeks had passed since he had left home.

After being beaten up by the Vega brothers, he had lain by the river. Then he had got up, recovered his rucksack and followed a track south. The track had led him into the Sierra Nevada. The wild landscape reflecting his state of mind. Bare and neglected. He wanted to tear out his hair. And howl and scream. Except that his body ached like hell.

Other times, he had felt numb. As if he was swathed in a mist. But he hadn't returned home. Instead, he had trudged on. Taking a path over the ridge back of the Sierra Nevada. To the other side. South. Where he felt calmer. A pleasant warmth coming up from the Mediterranean. Settling him down.

Since then, he had wandered. Living on nuts, berries and fruit mostly. Once, he had snared a rabbit. He had gutted it, stuffed it with herbs and chestnuts. Then he had roasted it over a fire. I ate the meal watching the stars come out one by one, he remembered.

He stood and surveyed the valley. Picking at a blackberry seed that had got stuck between his teeth. Far away, a single line of smoke was visible in the sky. It came from a farm house which was situated near a gorge and surrounded by almond and olive groves.

His gaze settled on the farm house. Watching the smoke rising up, he imagined a family sitting cosily inside, beside a fire. He observed the house in the valley a little more. Perhaps you have spent enough time alone, he thought to himself. So he adjusted his rucksack and headed in the direction of that place.

By the time Victor had made it to the gorge, the sun was dropping behind the mountains. And the clouds were shaded pink. A cold wind had picked up. A path took him past wild oaks whose leaves rustled on twisted branches. Their discarded acorns crunching under foot. Victor shivered, wanting to reach the house before it was dark. But unable to find a way across the gorge. It must be at least ten metres wide, he thought, peering down at a furious river, hoping there was a bridge downstream.

He carried on. Wondering what sort of people lived on the farm. I hope they are decent folk, he thought. Not freaks, like those two men from that café with no name. But you ran off without paying, he reminded himself. What did you expect?

Further along the path, a walnut tree was lying across the gorge. It had been blown over in a storm and its roots had been torn out. This is not exactly a bridge, Victor thought, wiping some sweat from his forehead. But I've got to cross somewhere.

The trunk creaked when he climbed on. All the same, he shuffled forward. Uncertain, unsteady. The wind tugging his body.

From the depths, the rumble of the charging water rose. But he didn't look down. He continued on, the rucksack on his back. Little by little, he thought. Bit by bit.

All the time, stones and dirt tumbled from the sides of the gorge into the vacuum below. Then the trunk groaned and rolled to one side. Victor lost his balance. One moment, he was on his feet. The next he was falling. Grappling with the air.

3
Blur

"Katy!" James shouted entering the house. He had been trying to get hold of her for two days now. But she wouldn't answer the phone. So he had picked up a spare set of keys and driven to Fulham. Now, he stood at the bottom of the stairs.

"Katy?" he shouted again, peering into the kitchen where dirty crockery and cutlery cluttered the sink. Next to it, a collection of wine bottles stood empty and there was a glass ashtray, overflowing with cigarette stubs.

James opened a window, letting in some fresh air. Toblerone, the cat, came in. There were some black and white photos of a young man pinned on a board. James looked at them. And then he ran his eye down a document on the sideboard below. He stood very still. Biting his lip.

Katy heard the footsteps climb the stairs. If only they would go away, she thought. They seemed to follow her everywhere. But this time it was not her imagination. The door to the bedroom slowly opened, letting some light in. Her father stood in the doorway.

“Katy, it’s almost midday,” James said. “What are you doing still in bed?” He drew the curtains so she raised a hand and shielded her eyes from the light. “And why don’t you pick up the phone?” James wanted to know, looking at the clothes scattered all over the floor. “We’ve rung a hundred times.”

Katy groaned and turned over. “Are you OK?” James asked moving closer, waving a hand in front of her. His voice had become gentler. She blinked but she still didn’t respond. It was as if he was talking from far away. “Can you hear me, Katy?” he asked. She nodded. “What’s happened to you?” The question span through her mind.

Some time later, she didn’t know how long, her doctor, a big woman with swollen ankles, came into the bedroom and asked how she was feeling. Katy, sitting on the edge of the bed, just shrugged. The woman produced a thermometer and checked Katy’s temperature. Then she asked a string of questions.

“This will help you sleep,” the doctor said afterwards, twisting open the cap of a bottle and giving Katy a pill. Katy put the pill in her mouth and swallowed it down with water.

“I found these,” Katy heard her father say to the doctor in the passageway.

“They look like amphetamines to me,” the doctor said.

“Are you sure?” James replied. “But I thought she had turned that corner long ago.”

Katy closed her eyes. She was already slipping away. Back down into the darkness.

When she awoke again, she lay for a moment. Her father was sitting in a chair opposite the bed. He was reading a book. He looked up. “How are you feeling?” he asked.

"Awful," she replied.

He studied her for a moment. "Well, you can't stay here," he said. "You're coming with me."

Katy found she couldn't walk properly. A walking stick, Richard had once used after twisting an ankle years ago, was still leaning against the wall in a corner. She picked it up. In the bathroom, she leaned on the sink and looked at her pale, drawn reflection in the mirror. Blood-shot eyes stared back. What a mess, she thought. Then she changed and packed an overnight bag.

Her father was waiting when she hobbled downstairs.

"And Toblerone?" she asked looking around for the cat.

"I'll come back for him."

"And I should tidy up," she added looking at the mess.

"That can be dealt with too," James replied.

After locking up, they walked slowly down the street together. A chilly, autumn wind tugged Katy's hair. Everything seemed different to her. It was like being a visitor to a place that wasn't clearly defined. A hazy place with smudged edges.

James' Volvo was parked at the end of the street. Katy climbed in while James put the overnight bag in the back. James got in, started the engine and drove off. As he drove out of London, he said: "Your mother's cooking lasagne. Your favourite." Then he talked about the weather. She wasn't really aware of his words. She moved a strand of hair from her face and tried to focus. But everything was a blur.

4
Mint, Rum and Cigarettes

"I heard your nephew went missing," Richard said to Mike. They were in a tapas bar. Mike was Fiona's brother. A big, bulky guy who was just over fifty with long, grey hair tied in a pony tail. And a slightly bent nose.

"That's right," Mike said. "The wolverine goes walkabout."

From the wall above, a different species of animal glared down: a *bravo* bull with flaring, glossy, black nostrils. There was other bull fighting memorabilia: swords, capes, Corpus Cristi posters - with their abstract depictions of women dancing Sevillana – as well as the lists of *torreros* and the dates they had fought the bulls.

"Runs in the family," Mike added, staring at Richard. Richard didn't look away.

"Does it?" he asked wondering if Mike had worked it out.

"Sure does," Mike said.

Richard picked up his beer. It was cool and slipped down easily. Just what I need, he thought.

Going into class that day, had felt like entering a war zone. But then again it was Friday: teenage hormone and energy levels were high.

"So why do you think he ran off?" Richard asked.

"Beats me," Mike shrugged. His face remained impassive. He knows I am Victor's father, Richard thought again.

"Leo's so childish," Fiona was saying to a red-head when she entered the bar. "Storming off like that. He just can't see my point of view. He won't see it."

"Like most men," the red-head remarked. Fiona laughed. The red-head, whose name was Susie, went up to Mike. They kissed. Meanwhile, Fiona sat down next to Richard but it was hard to say if she was happy to see him or not.

The rest of the evening was a blur of bars and drink. Richard talked to Mike and Susie and then Tanya, the assistant director of studies, and her husband José. After that, he found himself alone with Fiona although he wasn't quite sure how it happened.

At two in the morning, they were still together, dancing under a revolving globe in a night club. Richard was in a sort of trance: Fiona appeared to be moving in slow motion, flecks of light on her glowing face, her lips parted, her eyes bright. She raised her arms and clicked her fingers. Flamenco style.

When they finally embraced, he could feel the warmth of her body and he could smell her perfume. But then she started trembling and held him tight. He couldn't see but he knew the floodgates had opened and the tears were running down her cheeks.

Afterwards, they sat on a sofa. Two *mojitos* perched on the low table in front of them. "Feeling better?" Richard asked. Fiona nodded, wiping away the last tears with a handkerchief.

"It's been a hard month," she said. "Feels like everything is going against me. Victor's still missing, things aren't good with

Leonardo, the school's in debt. I really needed to lose my head tonight." She snuggled up to Richard. "You seem to be the only one who understands."

Ten minutes later, they were kissing. They broke off, got more comfortable and kissed again. This time for longer. She tasted of mint, rum and cigarettes. Afterwards, he really felt heady, as if he'd just downed another *mojito*.

"Would Katy mind?" Fiona asked.

"Do we have to talk about Katy?" he replied. "What about Leonardo?"

"That son of a bitch."

Richard had never been unfaithful although he had had numerous chances: the exhibition openings in London were full of attractive women who were single (for the night anyway, if not on paper) and had both money and time to spend. But he had somehow resisted their pull. Promising himself that he should sit it out. That Katy would recover and turn a corner. She hadn't though. Now she seemed so far away from him. And not just geographically speaking.

Richard and Fiona resumed kissing. And then he felt her hand move across his waist and slip beneath the elastic of his pants.

"I think that's enough," he said.

"I don't," she whispered in his ear.

5
El Cortijo de Buenas Aires

The man who came through the trees was an African. He was big and strong and had a large, round face. He was dressed in a coat, jeans and boots. For a moment, he stood at the edge of the gorge. Staring at the young man whose hands were clinging to a branch of the fallen tree. The youth's head lolling to one side like a puppet in the greyness of dusk.

The African carefully climbed on to the trunk. Staying on his knees, the wood groaning under his weight. "Quick," he said stretching out a hand. Victor barely had the strength to look up. Or grab the hand of the African man who pulled him up. He swayed, struggling to find his footing. Trying to keep his balance. The African pulling him. Both men tumbling to safety.

Afterwards, Victor sat on the ground, the rucksack beside him, rubbing his sore arms. It felt as if they had been pulled out of their sockets. The African chuckled.

"What's so funny?" Victor asked.

"*Hombre*," the man replied. "There's a bridge downstream."

The African was still laughing when they took a path away from the gorge. This joined a track. The track cut between rows of almond trees, just visible, in the dying light. They passed a sign that announced El Cortijo de Buenas Aires. Further on, a rusty tractor and a trailer were parked between a pick-up truck and a row of hen houses. The farm house was up ahead.

It was illuminated by an outside light. A big, gypsy woman was filling a Jerry can with water. "What you got Bouba Sarr?" she asked as the men approached.

"A live one," Bouba replied.

The woman looked at Victor, shook her head and went inside. Bouba Sarr followed the woman. And Victor followed Bouba Sarr.

In the hallway of the house, Bouba took off his coat and hung it up on a peg. Victor lowered the rucksack to the floor. Bouba took off his boots and put them with the other footwear. Victor copied him. They walked in their socks down a corridor. The smell of sizzling meat making Victor's mouth water.

In a sitting room, a group of men were sitting quietly around a fire. The men, immigrants mostly, turned and looked at Victor. Then they returned their gazes to the fire, its flames crackling in an open hearth. In a corner, a man with white hair was sitting in an armchair, reading a Bible. He was wearing a flannel shirt, corduroy trousers and thick socks. His name was Cayo Ortiz and he ran the farm.

"Look what we got here boss," Bouba said.

Cayo moved his glasses down the bridge of his nose and studied Victor.

"He almost got himself killed trying to cross the gorge," Bouba added.

"He did what?"

"He was hanging under that fallen walnut. I had to save his skin."

Cayo shook his head in disbelief. "What were you doing there son?" he asked.

"I fell trying to get to the farmhouse. I didn't know there was a bridge."

Bouba grinned. "I just told him."

"You was lucky," the man said.

Cayo Ortiz had been born in 1937. He was raised on the farm by his father and mother, along with eight brothers. None of them had gone to school. Julia, their mother - a kind but tough woman - had educated them. Teaching them basic skills: reading, writing and arithmetic. There wasn't much time for anything else.

From an early age, the children worked on the farm. Getting up at the crack of dawn. To harvest almonds and olives. To look after the farm animals. To respect and understand the seasons. To repair machinery. Cayo's father hadn't tolerated fools. And had been unforgiving.

One by one, his sons left home. They moved to the city. Until only Cayo was left. He married late, a gypsy girl called Dolores whose family came from a village not far away. She was twenty years younger than him. And she was strong. Cayo and Dolores took over the farm. Taking advantage of a new work force: young men, fresh from Africa, who were grateful for a wage (however pitiful), board and lodging.

Now, Cayo took a tooth pick from his shirt pocket and began chewing it. At the same time, he studied Victor. The lad was all skin and bones. He looked hungry.

"How old are you?" Cayo asked.

"Sixteen."

He wasn't sure how long Victor would last on the farm. But it was harvest time and another hand would speed things up. So he asked: "You looking for work *hijo*?"

6
Dew Cottage

Dew cottage was, in fact, a Georgian house. It had been built in 1820 and rebuilt in 1950. Wysteria and clematis now climbed the exterior, encroaching on the large windows at the front of the house as well as the elegant, white portico.

When the Volvo pulled into the gravel driveway Katy's mother opened the front door. Anne was a tall woman for her age. With a lined, stern face. Wearing a jersey dotted with faded Chilli peppers.

Anne came down the steps as Katy climbed out of the car. "I made the bed in your old room," she said giving Katy a kiss. Katy didn't seem to hear. Then Anne stood by James. Neither of them saying a word as Katy entered the house.

Katy slowly climbed the staircase. On the first floor, she leaned on the walking stick and paused to catch her breath. Her parents' bedroom, with its four poster, stood across the landing. Her sister's old room was on this floor too; now a spare room. Then she continued upwards. To the attic room.

It was still inhabited by her past. The cuddly toys, a bunch of old squatters, refused to leave the bed. A set of Beatrix Potter books occupied the book case. There was a globe lamp on the chest of drawers and a framed photograph of herself sitting at a piano. In another photograph, she and two hundred and fifty other girls stood in front of a Victorian building.

Anne came up the stairs with Katy's overnight bag. She entered the room and put it down and then sat beside her daughter on the edge of the bed. "Are you on drugs dear?" she asked. "Doctor Sheiland said that you've been taking MDMA and some other stuff."

"It was for pain relief."

Anne stared at her daughter. "Pain from what?"

From married life, Katy felt like saying. She didn't though.

Instead, she wondered what else Doctor Sheiland had told her parents.

"And why didn't you tell me you had a son?"

Katy looked down at the carpet.

"Oh that," she said.

"Yes, *that*," Anne replied. The older woman paused. Her eyes had narrowed and her mouth was turned down: "What on earth is going on?"

Katy took a packet of Marlboro out of her jacket pocket. Then she got up, hobbled over to the window and opened it. After she had lit up, she remained by the window, looking out over the garden as she smoked. The sky was a metallic grey. More rain was on its way.

"You gave him away didn't you?" her mother said coming over. Her voice had an accusing edge to it. Katy didn't answer. "I guessed," her mother added. "I knew. It was intuition. That time you came down from Edinburgh, you looked just how I had felt after giving birth." A clock ticked on a shelf. The rain pocked the window. “Of course, I never mentioned this to your father. He would have been furious if he had known you gave a child way. Anyway, it was too late to interfere.”

A tear rolled down Katy’s cheek. She didn’t feel relief at her mother’s knowledge. Quite the opposite. It was like salt being rubbed into a gaping wound.

*

“She’s in a right mess, isn’t she?” Anne said to James downstairs. They were sitting at the kitchen table. With cups of tea. The humming fridge providing a soft, background noise.

James nodded. “I can’t understand why she’s suddenly back on the drugs,” he said.

“I can,” Anne replied.

James didn’t seem to hear. He was looking at a shelf of books. Going back through the past. Trying to figure out why his daughter had taken this route.

Oncc, Katy had been a steady girl. Attaining good GCSEs and A levels, getting into Edinburgh university. She had not been like her sister, Deborah. A teenage rebel. Who had dropped out of college and ended up living in a commune in Dorset. But that hadn’t been for long. Somewhere down the line, Deborah had worked life out. She had gone back to college, found a job, married and settled down.

On the other hand, Katy hadn’t worked life out. It was like she had gone backwards. James turned to his wife. “Where did we go wrong?”

“I don’t think *we* have much to do with things any more,” Anne replied carefully. “Richard has stirred everything up. Running away to Spain to look for the boy, our missing grandchild, who it appears has gone astray once again. She lost the boy years ago and all evidence suggests she's on the point of losing the husband too."

7
In the Rain

When Richard woke up, Fiona was not lying beside him. But her side of the bed was still warm. And her clothes were hanging over a chair in the corner of the room. He lay for a moment, trying to remember the events of the previous night. But, like an incomplete puzzle, they did not fit together.

He scratched his chest. It was almost hairless and pale in the morning light. Then he kicked back the duvet and climbed out of bed. He scuttled like a beetle, naked and shivering, down the short passage, entered the bathroom and bolted its door.

A second later, Fiona appeared from the sitting room. She crept down the passage in the opposite direction to Richard. In the bedroom, she changed in a hurry. She could not find one of her boots but she hobbled out of the flat anyway. Slamming the door behind her.

Richard had a shower. Afterwards, he dried himself with a white towel. He left the shower room with the towel wrapped around his waist. “Fiona?” he called out going to the kitchen. She wasn’t there. Nor was she in the sitting room where the documents of Victor’s adoption, the agency report and its photographs lay scattered on the floor.

In the bedroom, he sat down heavily on a corner of the empty bed and cursed. The chair, where Fiona's clothes had lain, was bare but he could see a boot on the floor beneath it. She must have dressed in a panic and fled, he thought, picking it up.

He jogged down the stone stairs, carrying the boot, the towel still wrapped around his waist. On the floor below, a face peered through a crack in a door. Pilar, the nosey neighbour, he thought, continuing on. At the bottom of the stairs, he crossed the hall and stepped outside, onto the street. But the only people he could see were a respectable Granadino family. He grimaced - frightening the children who drew near to their parents - while imagining Fiona hopping across town.

Last night was hardly an erotic fantasy come true, he told himself later, in the kitchen. In fact, it's amazing that you managed to keep it up. In your drunken state, my friend, you were unfaithful to your wife. And now the mother by adoption, of your son, knows everything!

He wondered if Fiona would confess her sin to Leonardo. And tell him her discovery. I doubt it, he thought. All the same, I am not going to sit around all day waiting for an angry thump on the door. So he got changed and left the building. He walked down to the river and wandered aimlessly.

He boarded a bus which rumbled through town. Between endless blocks of flats, shops, bars and offices. It was hot. Richard was sweating alcohol. They went by Las Cármenes, the football stadium. Then the bus broke out of the city. Passing ploughed fields and olive groves. A timber yard and an empty factory. The bus stopped in a town. Then in another.

Richard got off at the end of the line. And walked through a seemingly abandoned village. Fallen chestnut leaves, curled brown and yellow, lay scattered or blown into piles by the wind on the empty streets.

At the end of one street, there was a café. He sat outside on its terrace. Still sweating alcohol. Some flies, visitors from summer who refused to leave, buzzed around the table. A cat snoozed in a corner. A waiter, whose face was pitted with scars, came over. Richard ordered a *caña.*

The *caña* came accompanied by a plate of cooked snails. Richard grimaced and pushed the plate of grimy looking molluscs away. He drank some of the beer. The cat awoke and came up to him. Richard threw it a snail which clattered when it hit the stone floor. He watched the cat paw the shell in an attempt to eat. But the dead mollusc kept rolling away.

Later, he wandered out of the village. Taking a path that ran between two ploughed fields. In a pine forest, he trod heavily on a blanket of dead needles. His breathing was heavy. Near by, fallen trees created a criss-cross of broken lines. It reminded him of a landscape by Paul Nash which hung in the Tate gallery. Instead of trees though, he recalled a quagmire of fallen planes, their wings at all angles. That desolate scene is somehow repeating itself here, he thought.

He trudged up a hill. When he reached the top, he stood facing Granada. The city's grey tentacles stretched out in front of him like those of a giant octopus. Behind, dark clouds hovered unannounced, an alien force waiting to strike. Rain drops fell, flecking his face and clothes. But he just stood at the top of the hill, somewhat glumly with his hands in his pockets, staring into space. Trying to comprehend how a lost son and a broken marriage had led him to the heart of Andalusia.

Richard walked slowly back down the hillside. In the village, he waited for the bus. It was still raining. Across the other side of the road, coming through the open window of a house, Latin lovers were arguing on a TV show. There was the sound of crockery being smashed, a woman screamed and a man – Argentinian, perhaps – cursed obscenely.

8
Hard Labour

A pale, morning light filtered through the dormitory windows of El Cortijo de Buenas Aires. It illuminated the sleeping men on the beds. Only one of them had risen: Bouba Sarr, the African, was sitting cross-legged on a carpet. His face expressionless, like an Olmeca head.

After a while, he opened his eyes and yawned; his white teeth gleaming in his pink mouth. Then he stretched his arms and rose. While he changed into a pair of blue overalls, he looked over at Victor. The young man he had saved was sound asleep in the next door bed. Bouba shook his head. "Rise and shine kid," he said. Victor groaned. And dug deeper beneath his blankets. "I said rise and shine," Bouba hissed. "There's wood to cut!"

Outside, Victor rubbed his hands together and stamped his feet. His warm breath clouded the cold air. He felt drowsy as he followed Bouba to a wood pile. And stiff too. Bouba set a log down and quartered it with an axe. "Your turn," he said. Victor chose a piece of wood and picked up the axe. He raised it and swung it down. The blade lodged itself into the wood with a dull thud.

Bouba cursed. He pushed Victor aside and freed the blade. Then he sliced straight through the log. Afterwards, he glared at

Victor. "You ever cut wood before?" Victor shook his head. Bouba cursed again. "Get with it," he said. Then he shoved the axe back into Victor's arms. "We need three loads," he added pointing to a wheel barrow. "And hurry up or you'll miss breakfast."

When Bouba had walked away down the track, Victor placed another log upright on the ground. He lifted the axe over his head and drove it down hard but once again it got stuck. "Fuck," he said.

*

"Anything left?" Victor asked Cayo's wife in the kitchen of the house when he had finished chopping the wood. Dolores nodded towards the table.

"Late comers get the scraps," she grunted. Then she continued scrubbing a chopping board at the sink.

Victor went over to the table, grabbed a mug and poured in the dregs from the coffee pot. He added curdled goat's milk from a metal jug. In a basket, there were a few husks of stale bread. He put a piece on a plate and spread some butter on this. He was scraping a sticky tin for jam remains, when the bell rang outside.

"*¡Vamonos!*" a voice yelled. "*¡En marcha!*" It was Cayo so Victor hurried out. When Cayo saw Victor he shouted: "Hurry up, *¡hijo!* We haven't got all day!" The other workers were already climbing into the back of a pick-up, its exhaust spurting black fumes. Victor threw away the coffee, dropped the husk of bread - which one of Cayo's dogs wolfed down - and grabbed his jacket. Then he ran over to the vehicle.

Bouba helped Victor climb into the back. But when Victor sat down, he smacked the back of his head on a rail. Groaning in pain, he rubbed the swelling; it hurt like hell.

Two workers grinned, shaking their heads. "You really won't last long here kid unless you wake up," Bouba warned.

Cayo put the vehicle in gear and the pick-up bumped down a track, heading east, between rows of almond trees. Bouba took out an aluminium foil wrap with some strips of salted cod inside. He offered one to Victor. Victor shook his head. Bouba shoved a piece in his hand anyway. "You'll need it," he said. Victor chewed on the salty cod. It made him thirsty but he didn't spit it out. Behind, Cayo's dogs followed at a steady lope, their pink tongues hanging out.

*

That evening, Victor sat at the dining table with the other farm hands. The polished table was worn and pockmarked and the chairs that accompanied it were of wood or plastic and different colours like the men who sat on them. Everyone was hungry. They had been harvesting the almonds all day, only getting a short break for lunch. And it had rained so the ground became heavy and the boots of the workers, that had been left in the hall, were all caked with mud.

Dolores carried a blackened pot into the room. She lowered the pot on the table and began ladling out the contents into bowls.

"What we having mama?" Bouba asked.

"Meat and veg stew," Dolores replied.

Victor looked eagerly down at his bowl and saw fatty morsels floating in oily sauce. Even old dog would taste good, he thought with a shrug, digging in.

As he ate, he listened to the others: Bouba talking about Dakar, Senegal. Naazhim, from Morocco, bringing up the Middle

East. Blaming the Americans for the extended conflicts. And defending Russian foreign policy. Omar, Naazhim's cousin, a skinny guy, disagreeing. Calling the Russians power hungry. And seekers of turmoil. The others in the room listening. Some nodding. Not Cayo, Dolores's son though. Eduardo ate in silence. He was a big man who was deaf.

At the end of the meal, Cayo talked about what needed to be done the next day. Victor listened, feeling drowsy. His eye lids heavy. Then everyone got down from the table. Victor went to the dormitory and lay on his bed, listening to the noise of chatter coming from the sitting room. And the crackle of wood burning in the fire place.

From the kitchen, he could hear Dolores washing the dishes. Further away, outside the house, the river gurgled down the gorge. Someone lit a match and cigarette smoke wafted in. Victor thought of his parents smoking after the evening meal. He pictured them standing on the porch, watching the gate. Waiting for him to return home.

9
The Wellhouse

They were sitting around a fire. Flames flickering and dancing. Katy's eyes went from one face to the next. Searching: a man, a woman, Richard.

Richard was gazing at the woman. She turned to him and smiled. While the man slowly took a flick knife from his pocket. He clicked it open. Then the man grabbed Richard but it wasn't Richard any more. Victor had taken his place. The man raised the knife triumphantly. Then he plunged it down.

In the bedroom, Katy jolted upright. Her cry fading. She was sweating. And her heart was beating fast. She rubbed her eyes. Waiting for the nightmare to subside. This one, she knew, had been much more vivid than the last.

*

That afternoon, Katy left Dew cottage. James drove her through Twickenham. Then down the M3. Despite the fact that the car was going at 70 mph, things were moving slowly in Katy's world. She was under sedation. So the road signs seemed to float past the car. Or is the car floating past the road signs? she wondered.

She had been living with her parents for three days. But her health hadn't improved. In fact, it had got worse. She had stayed in her room and barely touched the meals brought up for her. James and Anne had managed to persuade her she needed professional help.

James turned off the motorway and they went down a country lane. Prickly hedgerows blocking out the world. They followed signs to The Wellhouse whose long driveway was dotted with oak trees. Beneath the trees, there was a mottled carpet of yellow and brown leaves.

James slowed at a gate and pressed an intercom. The gate opened. The car rattled over a cattle grid. A building came into view. It loomed huge and grey. Tyres crunched over gravel. James parked. Katy looked up at the barred windows on the façade of the building and shifted in her seat. It's like going back to boarding school, she thought queasily.

James had told her that The Wellhouse was founded by Doctor Edward Bainbridge. Doctor Bainbridge had been married to a woman whose maiden name was Eleanor Cartwright. They had three children. The eldest child, Robert, had suffered from schizophrenia. Because of this, Doctor Bainbridge dedicated his life trying to decipher mental illness.

He travelled round the world and met the most respected doctors in the field. He learned about depression, anxiety, learning disabilities and mood disorders. About phobias, obsessive-compulsive disorders and addictions. He studied psychotherapy, psychoanalysis and cognitive behavourial therapy.

In India, he visited a hospital run by Tibetan monks. They ran a programme which centred on the well-being of each patient.

Helping both mind and body. Dr. Bainbridge's treatment mixed organic elements with mainstream medicine. The word 'organic' had never impressed James but the Wellhouse had a good reputation. And the staff were highly qualified.

Father and daughter got out of the car and made their way silently to the building. Katy used her walking stick to steady herself. Inside, a faint smell of disinfectant mixed with boiled vegetables so Katy wrinkled her nose.

They went up to the desk at reception. The receptionist welcomed them. Her name was Gail. Gail wrote down a few of Katy's details. Afterwards, Katy and James sat in the waiting room. Katy didn't speak. She stared at lime green walls. Then down at the carpet. And finally, at a pile of National Geographic magazines lying on a table.

Five minutes later, a nurse appeared. She had short, blonde hair and a peculiar, a lop-sided smile. This was because one side of her face had been squashed in a car accident. Her name was nurse Jacks. She talked to James and Katy (she had a speech impediment but it wasn't severe) before she led Katy away down a long corridor decorated by paintings of wild flowers.

Katy looked over her shoulder. She could see her father standing at the entrance. His white hair shimmered in a halo under the neon lights. She wanted to pull herself free of nurse Jacks and run back to him. But she was firmly guided on, round a corner, deeper into the building. They passed a door with 'Quiet Room' written on it. Then a music room.

"Here is your room," nurse Jacks said stopping outside door number 108. It was in the Robert Bainbridge Wing. The room was sparsely furnished: a single bed, a bedside table, a chest of drawers, a desk and chair. Through a window, there was an enclosed gravel courtyard where a slender olive tree stood.

Katy put her overnight case by the bed. “If there is anything you need, just call,” nurse Jacks said pointing to a phone. Katy nodded. The door made a click when nurse Jacks left. Katy tried the handle but the door wouldn’t open. She was locked in.

10
Down by the River

"You left this in my flat," Richard said placing a plastic bag down on Fiona's desk when he walked into the Newman School of English on Monday morning. Fiona was sitting alone in her office. She peered into the bag, saw her boot and quickly put it down, behind the desk. Out of sight.

Then, as if nothing had happened, she carefully tore open a sachet of sugar and poured the contents into a steaming mug of coffee. Some of the grains sprinkled over the surface of the desk, bouncing around like atoms.

"I don't normally go through people's stuff," she said. "But I knew you were hiding something. When I found the detective agency report, the photos of Victor, the copies of the birth certificate and adoption forms, I might have throttled you. Instead, I got changed and rushed out of the flat." She stared at him. "I had a hunch something was up the day I saw you. Why didn't you tell me you were Victor's father? You called yourself Brown. How long did you think you could get away with that?"

"Have you told Leonardo?" Richard asked.

Fiona shook her head. "Not yet. He's away."

Richard looked through the office window to reception.

"Can we talk somewhere?"

On a bench, down by the river, Richard told Fiona the whole truth. He started from the beginning. He told her about Katy's unexpected pregnancy while at Edinburgh university and the decision to give Victor away. He told her about breaking up with Katy and moving to London. Then getting back together and marrying. "We tried to have more children but a doctor told us it was impossible. Katy's womb was damaged as a result of Victor's birth, which had been complicated. Katy was crushed. She kept saying it was divine justice. That now we were being punished for giving a child away."

"After that, she became depressed. While I struggled to keep the gallery afloat. We simply drifted apart. So I decided to find Victor. I thought we needed a miracle of sorts. But Katy didn't like the idea. I left home anyway. When I arrived in Granada, I went straight to your house but you weren't there. The next day I followed you and Leonardo to the school. I was going to spill the beans when I entered but I just couldn't. That was when I made up the bullshit about looking for a job."

They got up from the bench and walked along the river. They passed the café restaurant, Kiosko Las Titas. They continued on, towards La Bola del Oro sports complex. Now Fiona spoke of her life, saying that she and Leonardo had adopted Victor because Leonardo was infertile and couldn't have children.

"We adopted in the UK because he didn't want anyone to know," she continued. "He said if his family and friends found out, they would make fun of him. It's the bloody Spanish *macho* thing. I told him not to be so silly but he begged me to keep it a secret. As a result, everyone in Leonardo's family thought I had given birth to Victor."

She gazed across the river at the plots of land on the other side. "Then we came to Spain. And when it was time to tell Victor the truth, I couldn't. If I did then Leonardo's secret would be out in the open. But I let it slip at a friend's house last year. I was drunk. Word slowly spread. So Victor found out anyway." Fiona fumbled in her pockets for a tissue. Richard stood there, feeling awkward. Then she turned and cried in his arms.

Later, when Richard had parted company with Fiona and was walking back to his flat, his mobile phone rang. He looked at the screen. It was his father.

"Have you phoned Katy?" the older man asked.

"She won't pick up."

"Don't you have the Wellhouse number?"

Richard paused. "Wellhouse?" he heard himself saying.

"Are you not aware that your wife has been admitted into a mental institution, Richard?"

For a moment, Richard was unable to speak. The events of the morning had left him sapped of energy. And now this. "But I thought she was with her parents."

"She was."

Richard didn't know what to say.

"Well do you want the number or not?" his father repeated.

Back in the flat, Richard stood on the balcony with a bottle of DYC whisky for company. A sprinkling of snow had fallen on the mountains far away. The sun was at its peak in the sky. High noon, he thought solemnly, looking down at the tiled floor that lay half in shadow. Then he lifted the bottle of whisky and drank.

11
A Dangerous Journey

The labourers were sitting in the living room of El Cortijo de Buenas Aires, facing a blazing fire. Some were chatting, others reading or snoozing. On the radio, a flamenco singer wailed a *cante jondo*. Everyone was tired. Not surprisingly, Victor thought, walking over to a table where Bouba was standing. We filled two entire trucks with almonds. He had filled out a bit and most of it was muscle. He lifted a kettle and poured some hot water into a cup.

"I used to dream of seeing snow," Bouba said looking out of the window at the white caps on the top of the hills. "Now I hate the stuff when it comes."

"I know what you mean," Victor said. "Winter must be hard here."

"It sure is," Bouba replied.

Victor added a tea bag, sugar and stirred his tea.

They sat at a table by a shelf of well-thumbed magazines and paper backs. Bouba opened a chess board and flipped the lid off a box of pieces. Then he picked up the black king and handed it to Victor. "You can be the nigger today," he said.

Five minutes later, Victor was check mate. It took Bouba just seven minutes to beat Victor in the second game. The third game lasted four minutes. During it, Victor watched Bouba move, trying to decipher his strategy but he just couldn't work out what was going on in the man's head.

"I think I'm going from bad to worse," he said.

"You just need to practice," Bouba said.

"I need an easier opponent," Victor corrected with a smile.

Later, they watched the news. There was some footage of would-be-immigrants trying to climb the wall in Ceuta.

"It must have been difficult to leave Senegal," Victor said.

"Hardest decision of my life," Bouba replied taking some photos out of his jacket pocket.

He showed them to Victor. In one, his wife was standing in a field at sun set. In another photo, the family were sitting on the steps of a shack. In a third, the children were playing on a dusty track.

"I left at dawn when they were all asleep," Bouba said. "I couldn't bring myself to say goodbye."

Victor remembered leaving too. "I didn't say goodbye either," he said.

Someone got up and put another log on the fire. The flames made patterns on the wall.

Bouba told Victor about his journey to Spain. After leaving his village, he boarded a bus and went to a city called Kébémer. From there, he joined a convoy of vehicles travelling to Morocco. They had to cross Mauritania. But they were stopped at a check point. "We bribed the police to let us continue," Bouba said. Soon after this, a woman fell ill and had to be taken to a doctor. "In Zuérate."

After five days on the road, they made it to the Mediterranean sea. "The boat to Spain cost the rest of our savings," Bouba remembered. "We boarded one cold February morning. It was the typical story; there were too many people crammed on board. But we had decided to risk it because we were afraid that if we did not take this chance, we would never get across." He paused, shaking his head at the memory.

"At first, we made some good progress. But then, dark clouds appeared on the horizon and the wind suddenly picked up. One moment, the sea was calm and the next, huge waves were crashing all around us. A storm was upon us. Three people were washed over board and the ocean swept them away in a second." Bouba was silent for a moment in respect for the trio who had lost their lives.

"After the storm passed," he continued. "We all huddled together to fight off the cold. And drifted. Then, as the sun was about to set, the silhouette of a coastline could be made out. We paddled as hard as we could but it was really the hand of God that pushed the boat towards the shore.

When we arrived, I remember kneeling down and kissing the sand of a deserted beach and thanking Him. For me, it was an incredible moment." The African was smiling now. "Destiny brought me here," he said. "One day, my wife and kids will follow. Then we will be united again."

Victor smiled. He hoped Bouba's dream would come true. Then he wondered when he would be ready to return to Granada and reunite with his parents. If I can still call them parents. Or should I look for my biological mother and father?

*

The next day, Victor and Bouba built a fence together. It was tough work. They had to dig holes in the hard, stony ground and lug metal posts up a slope. Victor soon felt tired but Bouba kept going. He told jokes and kept Victor's spirits up. When they returned to the farm house in the late afternoon, they took off their boots and hung up their coats in the hall.

Victor could smell meat and potatoes cooking in the kitchen. In the sitting room, the fire had been lit. Bouba went over to a table and began sifting through the post. The African paused for a moment and then triumphantly waved a blue, air mail letter in the air.

Victor smiled and went to pour himself some tea. He thought it would be good to get news from home. But when he turned to sit down by his friend, Bouba had already left.

12

Doctor Kernowe and Doctor Mann

"Here we are," nurse Jacks said stopping outside the door of a consulting room on the morning after Katy's arrival. Katy leaned on her walking stick. She was out of breath. The nurse looked at her watch and then knocked on the door.

Inside the room, it was quiet. Leather bound tomes filled the shelves of two enormous bookcases. Some framed portraits in charcoal of Greek philosophers hung on the walls. A tall lamp stood in a corner.

To one side of the room, there was a large, mahogany desk. Behind this, sat two men. One had curly hair and wore burgundy-rimmed glasses through which enquiring eyes shone. Dr. Kernowe, Katy thought. She had seen his photograph in the Wellhouse brochure. "Welcome Katy," Dr. Kernowe said. "Take a seat."

As Katy did this, she was aware of the other man silently studying her. This man was dressed in a pale blue suit. His thin blond hair had been carefully combed and was parted to one side and the clear, blue eyes that were observing Katy seemed strangely cold.

"So Katy," Dr. Kernowe said. "How are you feeling? A little lost?" Katy nodded. "That's to be expected. Did you sleep well? You should have done so." Kernowe looked down at some notes. "You were given some diazepam. How was breakfast?"

"She didn't have any," Doctor Mann interrupted. "Nurse Jacks informed me."

Katy flinched. Mann's tone was different from Kernowe's. It was clipped and aggressive, the voice of an interrogator.

Doctor Kernowe frowned. "You'll have to have some lunch," he said. "It's important to keep a good diet. You understand that, don't you Katy?"

Katy nodded.

"Good," Dr. Kernowe smiled. "That's settled then."

After this, Doctor Kernowe asked if Katy understood why she had come to the Wellhouse.

"To get better I suppose," Katy replied.

"So you understand that you're ill?"

"Yes."

"Do you want to get better?" Doctor Mann interrupted.

"That's why I'm here," Katy said.

"So what's wrong exactly? We have a note from a doctor." Doctor Mann paused. "Doctor..." He turned a page of a report in front of him. "Here we are, Doctor Sheiland. She says she put you on a course of anti-depressants a month back. Yet she found amphetamines and MDMA in your house. And a substantial number of empty bottles of alcohol. Are you an alcoholic?"

When Katy didn't reply, Doctor Mann continued: "On one occasion, you were found on a street corner at six in the morning. Did you often wander the streets in the early hours of the morning?"

Katy still didn't speak.

Doctor Mann closed the folder. Then he turned to Doctor Kernowe and shrugged like a lawyer who felt there was no point in continuing the case.

"Look Katy," Doctor Kernowe said in a gentler voice. "We want to help you so we need the facts. It seems you stopped taking a course of prescription drugs. Then you started consuming illegal drugs and large quantities of alcohol. Those substances have upset the balance of chemicals inside your brain. That's why you don't feel well and you can't walk properly. Now, it's our job to rebalance things. We're going to prescribe some new drugs to get the balance right. When you're better again, you can go back home. Do you understand?"

Katy remained silent.

Doctor Kernowe shifted in his seat. "Do you understand?" he repeated.

"Whatever," Katy replied.

"Will you have some lunch?" nurse Jacks asked in the corridor afterwards.

"If I feel up to it," Katy said. She was leaning on her walking stick, feeling agitated, itching for a fag.

"I don't think you understand," nurse Jacks said. "All patients must eat three meals a day."

"Must they?" Katy's eyes narrowed to slits.

"Yes," nurse Jacks said. "So we expect to see you down in the canteen later, OK?"

Katy hobbled back to her room alone. Inside the room, she sat at the desk. There was a pencil on it. It had *Get Well at the Wellhouse* stencilled on the side. She picked it up and wrote 'HELP' on a notepad. But her handwriting was almost illegible; the scrawl of a three year old.

13
Count Dracula

It is the hour of the *siesta*. And Richard is lying on the sofa in the sitting room of his flat. In his mind, a silent film is in progress. A huge, ogre-like nurse is clumping down a hospital passageway. She has a terrifying face. And she is holding a syringe in her left hand. Katy, wearing a torn white dress, shrieks in horror and backs away. But there is no escape: the woman grabs Katy and plunges the syringe into her thigh.

Katy is then dragged, screaming down a passage. She is pushed into a shower room where she is stripped naked and hosed down. Then she is made to sit on a chair. Her head is shaved. And the nurse (who is from Siberia) nicks her skull here and there (for dramatic effect). After that, Katy is pushed unceremoniously into a padded cell. Where she curls up, naked in a corner, and cries.

I have reduced my own wife to a dribbling wreck, Richard thought as he got up from the sofa, his clothes damp with sweat and his brow glistening. In the kitchen of his flat, a bottle of DYC whisky was standing on a sideboard. But what can *I* do? he asked himself, picking up the bottle and finishing the remains.

That day, a virus wormed its way into the art dealer's body. By nightfall, the enemy microbes had multiplied and were running wild in his blood stream. His temperature rocketed. He slept fitfully, his dreams an extension of his last waking thoughts: Katy is locked away again but no longer in a hospital. She has been transported to the highest tower of a Gothic castle. It is controlled by Count Dracula and his evil forces.

Only Richard can save her but he is sitting in a nearby pub and seems barely up to the task with no garlic, stake or crucifix. He doesn't even have a horse on which to gallop to the castle. But he decides to do the honourable thing: he trudges, bare-footed, through a thorn infested forest - wearing just a t shirt and shorts - in the pouring rain.

As he nears the castle, the ground becomes muddier and muddier. Katy's shrill screams can now be heard. But the gates are locked. He can only peer through them. A caped figure is at a window. When Richard zooms in on the creature's face, he cries out. Because the monster is him.

*

The next morning, Richard lay in bed, defeated. He was shivering and sweating at the same time. Outside, a cold wind blew over the city. He slept and woke and slept again.

When he awoke, he coughed and hacked and stared up at the ceiling.

The ceiling is like my life, he thought. On first impressions, nothing appears to be wrong. But when you look more carefully, a myriad of tiny cracks are visible. Then a fissure becomes apparent. Followed by a rent, a split, a fracture, a rupture. There are crevices and clefts. Fault lines meet. Gullies become canyons and chasms yawn. So, inevitably, everything will collapse around me. And I will crumble into nothing.

He rose, coughing, and hopped out of the room, over the cold tiles to the loo. His urine was the colour of burned nicotine. He turned on the tap and drank some water. Then he returned to the bed and pulled the blanket over him. His mobile rang a couple of times but he didn't get up and answer it. Then someone rang the doorbell. But he just lay there, his face a ghostly white.

14
Looking for Bouba Sarr

"Bouba! Bouba!" Victor shouted, going down a track, his torch beam breaking through dusk's veil, his footsteps crunching on frost. The African hadn't come back inside since receiving the air mail letter that afternoon. And now it was getting dark. Victor shivered and put a hand in a pocket. Then he continued on. A grunting noise made him swing the beam. A large form was crouched beside a tree. It wasn't Bouba though. A wild pig with wide, glaring eyes turned and charged away into the undergrowth.

"Bouba's missing," Victor said when he returned to the house. Cayo, who was sitting at the kitchen table repairing a watch, just raised an eyebrow and said: "He probably went down to the village to drink."

Victor shook his head. "On foot, in this weather? I don't think so. Anyway, Bouba doesn't drink."

"Well, you wouldn't know," Cayo replied. "You weren't here last year."

"What happened last year?"

"Let's just say that he had a few binges. We found him one time sleeping in a gutter."

Victor didn't believe it so he talked to some of the other men. They confirmed the story. Later, Eduardo, Cayo's deaf son, drove down to the village. It had two bars. But Bouba wasn't in either of them.

Victor kept on waking up during the night. And checking to see if Bouba was back. But the African's bed remained empty. And the next morning, Bouba was still missing. His bed undisturbed since the previous day. Some of his clothes were neatly folded on a chair. Other clothing was packed in a wooden chest under his bed. Along with his personal items.

At breakfast, Victor asked if they could all search the farm. "You've got an hour," Cayo grumbled. "And I will dock your pay." Even so, everyone put on jackets, hats and gloves and went outside.

Once again, frost crunched under foot. Victor's breath was cloudy. He clapped his gloved hands. "Bouba!" he shouted. The others were shouting too. Victor headed down a path to the gorge. He walked along its edge, scanning the bottom. The fallen walnut tree he had once climbed was lying there in pieces. There was something else down there too.

Victor managed to climb down. Then he scrambled over the rocks. When he arrived at the splintered tree, he stood for a moment, panting. The African was lying face up. His eyes staring up at the sky. Blood had dribbled from his nose and congealed on blue lips. Frost had frozen his hair and clothes. Broken shards of glass twinkled on the rocks. So did the neck of a whisky bottle. Victor knelt down. And closed Bouba's eyes. Later, he checked Bouba's pockets for the air mail letter. But it wasn't to be found.

15
Freak Central

Katy was sitting in the Quiet Room of the Wellhouse hospital, gazing through a window. At far away hills. She was remembering the day she had met Richard. It had been soon after her arrival at Edinburgh. On a university excursion. They had sat together on the coach. While they talked, butterflies had risen and fluttered uncontrollably around her stomach. She remembered the conversation, almost word for word. But I don't remember where we went, she thought.

The Quiet Room door opened and half a dozen patients poured into the room. Katy watched them swarm around the tea making area. Like flies, she thought. One overweight man noticed Katy. He turned and began making his way towards her. He had a large, puffy face and red, sticking out ears. And when he grinned, his crooked front teeth were visible. "We want you to be happy," he gasped raising a flabby arm. "We want you to be happy!"

Katy stared at the man. She knew his name was John Reynolds. John was a rock musician who had achieved fame and fortune. But it had gone to his head. So had large quantities of alcohol and drugs. As a result, he had wrecked his marriage and his career. Now, he was struggling to pull himself together in rehab.

"That's enough, John," a nurse said, coming over.

"I just want Katy to be happy."

"Sure you do," the nurse replied, patting his shoulder. John turned and swayed away, muttering.

The nurse was called Hans Teuling. He was a young man whose shaved head and narrow eyes gave him a mean appearance. He was strong too; the veins on his forearms and biceps bulged like the surface roots of a tree. Hans was a medical undergraduate from Eindhoven, Holland with a temporary work placement in the UK. He spoke with a slight Midlands accent because one of his uncle's was from Lincolnshire and Hans had a remarkable ability to imitate language. "Don't worry about John," he told Katy. "He doesn't mean any harm."

After the disturbance, another patient, came over. She sat down opposite Katy. Emily, the skinny woman from Sussex, Katy thought. Her long, wild hair, almost hid a mousy face etched with deep wrinkles. She wore a long grey dressing gown and bedroom slippers. She stared at Katy with wide open, wild eyes and then leaned over and whispered: "Once you're in here, you never get out."

Katy picked up her walking stick and rose. Talk about Freak Central, she thought hobbling out of the room and down the passage. Past the prints of flowers. Past the music room where a lonely piano sat, its lid closed. She didn't stop for a cigarette.

Inside her bedroom, she rested the stick against the wall. And tried to force open the window which looked onto the enclosed courtyard where the slender olive tree stood. But to no avail. So she sat on the edge of the bed. And attempted to control her breathing. Keep calm. Inhale through the nose and hold, she remembered from a therapy session. Exhale through the mouth. Pause. Again. Deep breaths. She screwed up her face. She released, relaxed and exhaled. She made fists.

WINTER

1
Encarnación

The old woman stood gasping at the top of stairs. One bony hand clutching the bannister. Under the other arm, a large box. When she knocked on the door, Richard appeared. Blurry eyed. And still in his pyjamas. "Come in," he said. But his landlady didn't need the invitation. She had already barged past him.

Richard shut the door and followed. Stepping over the chequered tiles on the floor in his socks. Shivering. Winter had arrived. The cold seeped through the windows and under the door. It crept into the rooms and stretched its icy fingers into every corner.

Richard shivered again when he entered the sitting room. He hadn't cleaned up the mess from the table: an ashtray full of cigarette stubs, an empty wine bottle, two glasses (stained a pinky red) and two dirty plates whose dry, yellowed remains revealed the paella he had cooked for himself and Fiona the previous night. Now, only the smell of the cigarettes and a faint aroma of perfume still hung in the air.

Things were going well with Fiona, he thought, despite clandestine circumstances. But perhaps it was those very circumstances which made their relationship worth its while: the couple enjoyed high risk encounters that were fun and brief. There was no time for melancholy or bitter regret.

At least not yet, Richard thought as he began clearing away the mess. Encarnación didn't seem to notice. She removed a large, metal disc from the box she had carried in, put this beneath the circular table and plugged its cable into a wall socket.

"What is that?" Richard asked.

"Just wait," Encarnación replied as a coil began to glow in the centre of the disc.

"Ah," Richard said. "An electric heater."

"Well done," Encarnación replied, her mouth forming a crooked smile.

Richard and Encarnación sat at the table with the table cloth covering their legs following their habitual ritual when she came for the rent money: he would make her coffee and she would tell him about the past.

"In the aftermath of the civil war, when I was a child, there was a lot of suffering," she told him that morning. "We were like sticks for a start. Not like kids today. I've never seen so many fat children. All they seem to do is watch the TV and stuff themselves with junk food! Our concern was survival. Every day was a struggle. We scoured the countryside for food. We searched for birds' eggs and wild fruit. We collected wheat and barley. Two of my sisters and one of my brothers died of tuberculosis. The youngest at three years old. My mother was heartbroken. But the doctors couldn't save any of them. There were few medicines."

"Do you blame Franco?" Richard asked, pushing his chair back, so he could move his legs (it felt as if they were burning) away from the heater.

"Not for that."

"But he did some terrible things, didn't he?"

Encarnación nodded. "He did. Or terrible things were carried out in his name. But of course, Spain was on its knees and there's no fancy way of pulling a country back together that has been choking itself to death. If you rip out a bad tooth with a pair of blunt pliers and without anaesthetic, blood is going to flow."

Encarnación then told Richard that she had been a member of Franco's state party women's section: "I was terribly proud of my sewing and motherhood achievements. But later, after my husband passed away, I became a liberal. I studied Philosophy at the university and even learned salsa. Now it's just a question of carrying out my last duties before I pass away. But I feel as if I have already failed in that. Why did my daughter fall in love with such an ugly, useless man? A half blind, fat hairdresser! After all her education! What does she see in Gonzalo?"

Richard thought of his neighbour. "Gonzalo's not so bad. In fact, he's kind and loving. Those are good qualities."

Encarnación's beady eyes seemed to harden like marbles. And her lips pursed. "Do you know what the problem with your generation is?" she asked.

"Tell me," Richard replied.

"You're soft and you're lost," she said. "You are lost because you have everything. You have nothing to discover and nowhere to go. As a result, you don't have ambition."

Richard looked at the veins that covered Encarnación's knobbly, bony hands. Then he looked into her hard eyes.

"I think you may be right," he said.

He tried the heater for a few days but he never found it satisfactory. So he gave up, went to a *ferreteria* and bought a couple of portable radiators which warmed the whole place up much more effectively. He also purchased two Moroccan carpets from a door-to-door salesman. One of them, decorated with gold, blue and red motifs, went by his bed; he hated starting the day by placing his feet on a chilly, stone floor.

2
Puerto Lobo

This is a whole lot better than that slosh Dolores served up, Victor thought, tucking into a juicy lamb cutlet on the terrace of a restaurant. A fortnight passing to the day, since he had discovered Bouba's body. He remembered the police coming and asking a lot of questions. The death was declared accidental. So Bouba was cremated and his ashes repatriated. Along with his savings.

Victor decided it was time to leave, guessing the police would inform his parents of his whereabouts. So he had packed up his belongings, said his goodbyes and walked off, heading east. Now, as Victor ate, an image of Bouba came to mind. Standing by an almond tree holding a basket, smiling.

After the meal, Victor leaned back in his chair and looked around. A young man was sitting at the next door table. He had dark hair and was wearing a Mexican style poncho, a pair of jeans and boots. The man took a pouch of tobacco and some papers out of a leather bag. He proceeded to roll a cigarette. Not an easy job with with just one arm, Victor thought.

When the man finished rolling, he lit up and puffed away, the smoke wafting in Victor's direction. "You staying or passing through?" he asked, looking at the rucksack at Victor's feet.

Victor thought the man was probably from Asturias by his accent. "I was going to go down to the coast," he replied. But now that he had tasted good food, he wondered whether he might hang around and added, "I like it here though."

The man nodded and smoked some more. "It's a good place," he said. His name was Plácido. And Victor was right, he did come from Asturias. In fact, he had grown up in a town near Oviedo. Now Plácido lived in Puerto Lobo.

"Is that another village?" Victor asked.

Plácido shook his head. "It's a community."

"What sort of community?"

"Oh, it's not religious if that's what you're thinking. We just work the land. Come and check it out. You might like it too."

As Plácido told Victor about Puerto Lobo, a young woman crossed the square. She had a good figure and moved easily. Her long, dark hair blowing in a breeze. She waved at Plácido who had stopped talking because Victor was gazing at the woman: "And it looks like you could do with company," the man added.

Victor and Plácido walked out of the village together. Following three people (which included the woman they had seen) and two dogs. They took a track through olive groves and then into a pine forest. Sunlight raking through the trees, creating small glades here and there. Ahead, a squirrel scurried across the track and the dogs gave chase.

Now a stream ran beside the track. The water splashing over rocks. Plácido knelt by the stream and filled a water bottle. He offered it to Victor. Victor drank. The water was clear, cold and refreshing. They walked on. Then the pine trees thinned out and Puerto Lobo came into view.

Victor and Plácido paused in a clearing and watched the group in front disperse over a hillside to the log cabins which were dotted over a terraced valley. Beside one of the cabins, a stocky blond-haired woman was tending a vegetable plot. Further away, a man and a horse were ploughing a field near where goats roamed.

"So, what do you think?" Plácido asked.

Victor was lost for words. Maybe, as a result of Bouba's death, he felt drained. Or perhaps he was simply relieved to have found new company. But it seemed to him, in that moment, he had finally arrived at a place that he previously thought only existed in dreams.

3
Fear and Violence

"May I join you?" a shrill voice asked so Katy looked up from the book she was reading on the sofa in the Quiet room. It was Emily again. The woman with bulimia. Her small, mouse-like face surrounded by wild, uncombed hair. Wearing her dressing grown and slippers. The sleeves of the former barely concealed fresh bandages circling her wrists.

"If you must," Katy said so Emily sat down opposite her. Although I don't want company, Katy thought. And why do you want to be with me anyway? I am overweight, my face is puffed up and I have fucked up. I feel like I am trapped in time, hiding in the darkness below decks of a battered, sinking boat while a storm rages and huge waves crash against the hull. She looked at Emily and added to herself. But perhaps you know how that feels?

Katy knew Emily had been force fed when she was a kid. Her mother tying her hands to the legs of chairs so she couldn't push the food away. And if she didn't eat, she would be locked in her room for the rest of the day. Or beaten by her father. Even so, Katy found it difficult to feel sorry for this peculiar woman. It was as if Emily had gone too far into the dark realms of insanity. How could she ever be drawn back?

Katy and Emily sat together in silence. Katy pretending to read but not really concentrating. Disturbed by this woman sitting opposite her. Emily looking at Katy as if Katy held some sort of key to recovery. As if she required something that Katy possessed but she was too afraid to ask for it.

Katy was about to close the book – it was a self help book that she was struggling to decipher - and say something when the door of the room suddenly flew open. John, the rock musician, and another patient, called Professor MacGregor, tumbled in. Emily and Katy retreated together. Backs against a wall. And watched, wide-eyed.

John grabbed hold of the professor. His hands clasping a skinny neck. His fat fingers squeezing. Katy watched his sweaty, red face, distort. She watched the fat on his cheeks wobble. The spittle on his chin. Then she watched Professor MacGregor choking and his pebble glasses falling to the floor. But Katy didn't move. She just stood there with her eyes wide open and her hand over her mouth. It was like something on television. Something that was not really happening in reality.

Then Hans Teuling rushed in. John was pulled off and pushed into a corner. One arm pinioned behind his back. Meanwhile, Professor MacGregor lay curled up, coughing on the floor. His pebble glasses broken. Katy looked at Emily. She was gaping. A dribble of saliva rolling down her chin.

Katy hobbled across the room, out the door and down the long corridor. Pausing by the music room. To catch her breath. The door was open and the piano visible. Its lid was open. But she just stood in the door way. Catching her breath. The image of John's angry face in her mind.

4
A New Assignment

Richard was alone in the staff room of the Newman School of English. He was studying a text book at the table, preparing a class in his head. He had made a cup of tea and the heater was on. He was remembering the start of term when his attempts to motivate a group of teenagers had failed. His chosen topics of discussion, songs and games had fallen flat and the students spent most of the class talking or day-dreaming. Anything but listen or contribute.

In one class, he had given up. He had sat down, placed his feet up on his desk and read a book. For a while, the students continued doing whatever it was they were doing. Chatting mainly. Then silence swept over the class. Richard looked up. Everyone was looking at him. Then someone asked him what he was reading.

It was a sci-fi novel. Someone asked him to read an extract. Everyone listened. In this way, he discovered that teaching teenagers was like training a shy animal. You had to let them come to you.

Now Leonardo walked into the staff room. Wearing a suit and tie, his hair carefully greased back. The smell of cigar and whisky on him. “I have been hearing things about you,” he said pulling up a chair.

Richard sat very still. So he’s found out about me and Fiona, he thought. Or that I am Victor’s biological father. Or both. Did Fiona spill the beans? Or did someone see us together?

“Don’t look so worried *hombre,*” Leonardo added. “It is good things that I have been hearing. Good things. The students like your classes. Even the teens and that’s saying something.”

Richard smiled in relief.

“That’s why we want you to teach at a secondary school,” Leonardo added.

Richard’s smile faded. “A secondary school?” he repeated.

“Right,” Leonardo said.

Leonardo pulled a flask from his jacket pocket and unscrewed the cap. “Fancy a drink?” He shrugged when Richard shook his head. Then he took a swig and put the flask back in the pocket of his jacket. “The school’s in X, in the north of the city,” he added. “Some of the students there need reinforcement.”

Richard had heard of X. Rumour said it was a marginalised area, run by street gangs and brimming with crime. “Are you sure I am the right person for this job?” he asked.

Now it was Leonardo’s turn to smile. Grin even. Whisky fumes in the air. “You are the only person for the job,” he said.

Richard cursed when Leonardo left the room. Then the bell went and students could be heard stampeding down the passage. Followed more quietly by their teachers who entered the staff room one by one.

Mike, Fiona's brother, was the first: "Fucking relative clauses," he cursed dumping his text books down on the table. "Which wear me out." He poured himself a mug of coffee and sat down.

Susie was next. She came in smiling. "One of my students leaned back too far on his chair and flipped over," she said. "Everyone split their sides." She opened the window, perched on the ledge and lit a Fortuna cigarette.

Ray Elfrick, a huge albino, was the third teacher to walk into the staff room. He placed his books on the table without a word. Then he sat down in front of the computer.

Tanya West, the assistant director of studies, was the last teacher that day to return to the staff room. "I gave them a composition to write," she said. "Only one person managed it." She opened the fridge and took out a Tupperware box. Inside, there was a sandwich wrapped in foil, a nectarine and a napkin.

Richard mentioned the new classes in X.

"The baptism of fire," Susie said, blowing cigarette smoke out of the window.

"We've all been there," Mike added. "You poor bastard."

Both Tanya and Ray were silent.

"Is X so bad?" Richard asked them. He felt flustered now.

Ray looked up from the computer and nodded.

"I'm sure you'll be fine," Tanya said.

Fiona came into the room. "What's up Richard?" she asked putting her books down. "You look in shock."

"Richard has just been told about his assignment in X," Susie explained.

Fiona brushed a hair from her face. "Oh, that."

"Yes, that," Richard said.

Fiona smiled: "It will be a great opportunity for you," she said.

*

Later, Richard and Fiona met in café bar Luna in the Realejo and sat together on a sofa with a glass of Ribera wine each. The illicit couple liked the bar because it was hidden down a side street and the dim lighting made it difficult to see people's faces.

Richard complained a little more about his new assignment.

Then Fiona told him that she and Leonardo had received good news. A policeman had told them that Victor had been working on a *cortijo* in the mountains, south of Granada, until recently. "Apparently, he's well," she said. "I feel so relieved."

"What work was he doing?" Richard asked.

"Farm work. Harvesting almonds and other stuff."

"But how did the police find out?"

"Apparently there was an accidental death on the farm so there was an investigation."

She cuddled up to him. They kissed. And again. Then they lay back and kissed some more. After that, Fiona talked about bringing up Victor in London. Richard wondered if he had ever seen them although he knew the possibility was remote in the extreme. Sometimes, on the London streets, he had studied the faces of children and wondered if he would recognise Victor's, the child he had once held.

"But Leonardo lost his job," Fiona said. "So we sold up and moved to Spain. We set up the school and then we bought the house. Victor has always been shy so he took a while to get used to things. But after he had made some friends at school, he was fine."

Richard smiled. "What about when he turned into an adolescent?" he asked. "What was he like then?"

"He spent a lot of time in his room. Reading. Or playing video games. That drove Leonardo mad," she continued. "So he tried to get Victor out. They went shooting together a couple of times in the foothills of the Sierra but Victor didn't think much of that. He didn't like the bull fights either and Leonardo's a big fan. The only thing they did successfully together was ski. They seemed to connect on the slopes somehow. But that connection was like the snow and always melted away."

Richard watched Fiona as she spoke. She looked relaxed, almost radiant. Not the exhausted woman she had met back in September.

After the drink, they went to Richard's place. Fiona made herself comfortable on the sofa while Richard poured whisky into a pair of tumblers.

"Do you like Stan Getz?" he asked turning on the stereo.

"Never heard of him."

"Dave Brubeck?"

She shrugged.

"How about the Duke?"

"Try me."

So Richard put on some Duke Ellington and they sat together on the sofa with their whiskies. Richard smiled. Things are looking up, he thought. Fiona was good company. Katy is in safe hands. And Victor was probably all right, where ever he was.

5
Estrella

Victor was writing a letter at a desk in one of the log cabins of the Puerto Lobo community. It was peaceful and warm in the cabin. There was an old clock on the wall (whose soft tick lulled him to sleep at night), a bed, a chest of drawers, a bookshelf and a wood burning stove. Some coal still glowed from the morning when it had been lit.

When he finished the letter, he folded it and tucked it into an envelope which he addressed to his parents and sealed. Then he stood up, put on a jacket and went outside. He walked down the path. Breathing the fresh air. Enjoying the warmth of the afternoon sun which illuminated the valley's terraces and flowing streams.

Someone was playing an acoustic guitar. It was Estrella. He had first seen her while chatting to Plácido, the one-armed Asturian, in the village restaurant. And he had been aware of her ever since. She was sitting on a fallen trunk. The guitar cradled in her slender arms.

"Hey there," he said going over.

She stopped playing and looked up. Long, black hair. A ring in her nose glinting. Dark, sad eyes.

"What's up?" she asked.

"Just off to collect the wood."

"Are you? How about I help you? Then you can help me cook later."

"Deal," he said stretching out a hand.

They collected the firewood in a copse of wild oak trees, east of the clearing, and loaded a rusty wheelbarrow with a flat tyre. Down here, there was a cabin surrounded by overgrown plants and various abandoned domestic appliances. In the summer, it was normally occupied by an old man called Ángel, who lived in Madrid, and co-owned the land along with his children.

Victor kept watching Estrella as she worked. She seemed in her element out here because he couldn't imagine her sitting in a classroom or working in an office. She was different to other girls. Almost animal like.

He knew only a little about her: that her parents were migrant workers and had once dragged her round Andalucia to help them with the various harvests: olives, oranges, broad beans, asparagus, strawberries, water melons, cherries, grapes, you name it.

At sixteen, tired of the itinerant lifestyle, she had left them. And gone to Cordoba where she worked in a factory, screwing the tops on perfume bottles. She worked as a cleaner in a hotel. Then as a waitress in a roadside café but one night the owner locked the doors and raped her.

After that, she lived for a while on the street. It was there she met Carlos Mendez. A thick set, muscular man with a shaven head. When she had told Mendez her story, he and some friends had driven to the roadside café and beat up the owner.

Mendez had taken Estrella to a commune outside Cordoba. He was an anarchist and demanded the liberation of the individual from the tyranny of state control. He and Estrella had marched in a number demonstrations in Madrid. They had taken part in night time riots. One night, Mendez had shot a police man, wounding him, and he was now a wanted man. Puerto Lobo was the perfect hide-out for him.

Victor did not like Mendez. Not just because Estrella was with him. Because he prowled around with a scowl on his face. Because he didn't do his chores or help anyone else. Because he spent entire days holed up in the cabin he shared with Estrella. Working on anarchist propaganda, apparently. The man is a time bomb, Victor thought. Slowly ticking away. Just waiting to explode.

"So what will it be?" Victor asked Estrella while heaving the loaded wheelbarrow back up the slope towards the centre of the commune.

"Pasta," she replied.

"What a Carbonara? Bolognese? Rigatoni?"

"Sorry," she laughed. "Just good old pasta with veg."

At the top of a rise, they paused and looked across at Puerto Lobo bathed in the evening light. It was a beautiful scene: the cabins in the clearing, the forest, the sound of the blackbirds going to bed. Except there was a lone figure waiting below. Victor frowned. Mendez: the blot on the landscape.

"I've been looking for you everywhere," Mendez said to Estrella when she entered the clearing. "Where have you been?"

"I was helping Victor collect the wood," she said.

Mendez looked at Victor. "Stay away from my girl," he warned.

"Or what?" Victor asked.

"You'll see," Mendez replied. Then he grabbed Estrella's hand and pulled her away.

6
If I'm Still Here...

The administration of medication at the Wellhouse was usually supervised by the nurses. They did the rounds each morning, lunchtime and evening, knocking on doors and making sure each patient took his or her correct dose.

But on this particular morning, Katy feigned swallowing a pill, dropping it down the sleeve of her jersey instead. Afterwards, when the nurse had gone, Katy flushed the pill down the toilet. Unfortunately, it was this particular pill that was helping to rebalance the chemicals in her brain. By the time she went to her appointment with Doctor Mann, she was feeling anxious and stressed out.

"This place is a mad house," she blurted out in the consulting room, even before she had sat down.

"We prefer to call it a hospital," Doctor Mann replied quite seriously. He was sitting across the other side of the desk with Katy's recent medical history open in front of him.

"Well, this hospital has some serious problems to solve. You must have heard what John, the rock star, did yesterday. Attacking another patient. That behaviour is not acceptable."

"I heard about the fight," Doctor Mann said. "It was unfortunate."

"Unfortunate?" Katy replied. "Is that all you have to say? What are you going to do about it?"

Doctor Mann observed Katy from across the table. His eyes were a clear, cold blue. "What do you propose we do?"

"John should be sectioned off. In fact, all patients should have individual areas. We shouldn't have to mix."

"Individual areas for all patients?" Doctor Mann said blinking in surprise.

"Yes," Katy said.

"That's isolation, Is that what you want? Total isolation in this..." he paused. "Mad house." Then he fixed his pale blue eyes once again on hers.

Katy looked down at her hands. They were folded on her lap. She stared at the red skin surrounding her finger nails. Shredded and raw. "No," she said. "I don't to be isolated but I don't want to be infected either."

"You are not being infected," Doctor Mann said bluntly.

"Well, that's what it feels like."

"Then you have to overcome it. You have to overcome your fears. Cutting yourself off won't help. Integration is healthy. It's important to learn to live and work with others."

Katy looked up. "Not when people like John are on the loose." When she spoke, her lips felt tight around her mouth and her voice sounded strained. She added: "I want to go home."

Doctor Mann shook his head. "Impossible. You're not ready."

He looked down at his note pad. "We are going to introduce a dose of Lorazepam into your medication. It is a benzodiazepine and should help to reduce your anxiety. Do you have anything to add Katy?"

"I want to see Doctor Kernowe."

"You know he's away today."
"Then tomorrow."
"As you wish."

He scribbled something down. "You have another appointment with me in a couple of days. On Thursday at ten. Will you attend?"

Katy's eyes narrowed. "If I'm still here."

Doctor Mann frowned. Then he placed his elbows gently down on the table, entwining the slender fingers of his hands together. "Now Katy, what exactly do you mean by that?"

*

Afterwards, she picked up her walking stick and hobbled back to her room. She had quit smoking so she didn't stop on the way. She sat on her bed, brought her knees up and pushed them against her chest. She cursed herself for coming out with that comment. If I'm still here! And what *do* you mean by it, she asked herself. Are you going to break out? Or perhaps you want to do yourself in. Top yourself. Commit Suicide. Harakiri! She tried to laugh but she grimaced instead. Do you? Now, tears rolled down her cheeks and she shook her head and rocked backwards and forwards.

I will be at the top of Doctor Mann's list of fruit cakes now, she thought. She wondered who else was on the list. Emily, no doubt. And John. Fat John, someone nasty within her said. Surely, he would be there or thereabouts, with his violent outbursts and threats.

7
X

Teachers must be fair and firm and they must be able to delegate responsibility as well. But the real key to survival, Professor Matthew Barnes of Birmingham university argued in his introduction to A Teacher's Guide To Classroom Survival, is the ability to keep students motivated. If you can not motivate students, they won't engage. If they don't engage, they get bored. And if they get bored, the class falls to pieces.

Richard was reading the book in a bus. The bus route was from the city centre - with its elegant hotels, shops and café bars - to X. In X, there were no elegant hotels and shops. There were no expensive café bars. There were no monuments and no tourists. Just council blocks and empty streets. On one corner, a bar had been boarded up. In another street, graffiti smothered the lowered shutters of closed shops. Skinny dogs roamed, sniffing litter and pissing on the charcoaled remains of burnt-out vehicles.

Richard got off opposite the school. It was protected by a high, concrete wall. On the top of which, a jagged line of cut glass glinted. To serve what purpose? Richard asked himself. To stop intruders getting in or the students getting out?

He walked up to the gates. And rang the bell. The school porter swayed nonchalantly over. She was a muscular woman, who wasn't to be messed with, and a local celebrity of sorts on account of winning a number of trophies in regional wrestling competitions.

"*¿Que quieres?"* she asked.

"I've come to give English classes," Richard said.

"*¿Nombre?"*

"Brownlowe," Richard replied. "Richard Brownlowe."

She glanced at a list on a clipboard. "*¿Que?"*

Richard pointed to his name. She grunted, ticked a box and opened the gate.

Richard followed the porter across a playground and into the main building. They walked down a long passage. At the end of it, two cleaners were putting mops and buckets into a cupboard. When they saw Richard and the porter, they looked at each other and giggled. The porter rolled her eyes and swung her burly hips and ushered Richard into a classroom.

The classroom was functional. There was no decoration on the walls and no fancy equipment. Just a blackboard studded with holes. Some of the students were already inside. The girls wore cheap jewellery and make-up. They were chewing gum, chatting away. While the boys – in t shirts and tracksuit bottoms mostly - leaned silently back in their chairs.

One girl was sitting alone. Doodling. Her hair had been shaven. On the front of her T shirt, the words 'Punk's Not Death' could be read. Richard considered pointing out the grammatical error. But when she looked up and glared at him, the metal braces on her teeth glinting, he decided against it.

"*Buena suerte*," the porter said, standing there with her hands on her hips. "*Lo vas a necesitar*. You're going to need it." Then she turned around and left the room. Richard was not listening. He was looking at the bars that protected the windows. And he was wondering why he had come to this hell hole.

8
Unwelcome Visitors

Victor and Plácido were standing in the shaded gully of a pine wood, two kilometres away from the Puerto Lobo community. Looking for *setas*, wild mushrooms. "Should be some around here," Plácido said prodding the ground with a stick. Victor knew Plácido had an impressive knowledge of flora and fauna; he often brought edible roots and plants, which Victor didn't even know existed, back to the camp.

The empty sleeve of Plácido's jacket swung as the Asturian squatted down and brushed some pine needles off a cluster of rusty pink mushrooms. He inspected them carefully before placing them in a basket. Victor knew that picking a toxic variety could be dangerous, even fatal.

Victor followed Plácido down the gully. They came across some fresh deer prints bordering a puddle of water. Then a large swathe of upturned earth where a wild pig had been rootling. He thought about his father, remembering their hunting trips together. Leonardo teaching him how to shoot rabbits, partridge, quail. Looking forward to Victor moving on to bigger game, wild boar. But his son had been a reluctant pupil. And, to Leonardo's irritation, a wayward marksman.

*

A string of explosions echoed down the valley as the two men arrived back at Puerto Lobo. Both stopped in their tracks. Plácido crouching as if preparing for battle.

"What's going on?" Victor asked.

"Beats me," Plácido said.

Then they continued. Outside one of the cabins, Estrella was taking some clothes off a line.

"What was all that noise?" Victor asked walking over.

"Some friends of Mendez have rolled up," she said holding the basket of clothes against her hip. "They brought some heavy duty firecrackers with them. Scaring the kids and the animals. Looks like they'll be staying for a while too."

"You don't sound too happy."

"I'm not. They're trouble."

Victor remembered Estrella telling him about Mendez's exploits with his anarchist friends. Mendez wounding a policeman in a riot and coming down to Puerto Lobo with Estrella to hide-out. "Are they really that bad?" he asked.

Estrella picked up a shirt. "Yes," she replied so Plácido chuckled.

Estrella put a hand on a hip. "Just wait until you meet them," she warned. Her face softened when she looked back at Victor. "A good crop of mushrooms," she said signalling to the basket.

"Sounds like we might need them," Victor said.

"*Si*," Estrella said. "Those pigs will scoff the lot."

Victor gazed at Estrella and wondered if he was falling for her. Whatever was happening, felt unsettling yet exciting at the same time. It was as if he had boarded a fair ground ride that was already in motion, there was no turning back.

In the clearing, Mendez and the visitors were standing around a fire. Beers and joints in hand. Light and shadow flickering on their faces from the flames. The smell of the firecrackers still in the air, mixing with marijuana.

One of the men, his name was Arsenio, watched as Victor and Plácido approached. Arsenio was an impressive figure. He was six foot two and weighed in at 190 kilos. As he studied Victor and Plácido, the silver ring which pierced the septum of his nose, glinted. "Who the fuck are these two?" he asked when Victor and Plácido were close enough to hear. "Little Red Riding Hood and the one armed bandit?" Mendez and the others burst out laughing.

The remark irritated Victor and he tensed but Plácido rested his hand on Victor's arm to calm him. "I hope your friends aren't going to cause problems," Plácido said to Mendez.

"They might," Mendez replied.

"And if we do," Arsenio added. "I wouldn't try getting in our way."

9
Deborah

Katy was feeling anxious. She hadn't slept well and she had barely eaten any breakfast. She was dreading the prospect of another day in the Wellhouse. Fruit Cake City, she called it. Or Freak Show Hell.

She looked down at a book on her lap she had been trying to read. It was a biography she had borrowed from the Wellhouse library about of a female politician from Africa who had started life in a tribal village. When the village was attacked by gunmen, the woman – just a girl at the time - escaped to the jungle, surviving on a diet of fruit, lizards and insects.

Katy frowned and closed the book. Then she hobbled round the room. There was a knock on the door. She opened it. Nurse Jacks was standing outside. "Your visitor's here Katy," she said.

The woman standing behind the nurse was the same height as Katy. Their faces were similar too. But this woman had wavy blonde hair and was wearing a leather jacket, a corduroy skirt and boots.

"Deborah," Katy said stepping forward. When they embraced, Katy closed her eyes and pressed her nose into her sister's jersey.

It smelt of perfume and family and pets and a little bit damp, but mostly of a reality she knew she had left behind.

"Funny how things have changed," Katy said when they were sitting on the bed in the hospital room. "When we were younger, it was you who was always getting into trouble."

"Don't remind me. You were so good. Mum and Dad always said that I should learn by your example."

"And now look at me," Katy said. "I've ended up in a loony bin."

"Well, you could be in the slammer," Deborah replied.

Deborah reached into her bag, took out a present and handed it to Katy. Katy stared down at the wrapping paper on which numerous cartoons dogs chased cartoon cats round in circles.

"Go on, open it," Deborah urged. "It's from Dave."

Katy tried but her fingers, bitten-to-the-quick, struggled to peel back the adhesive tape.

"He thinks Selotape's for keeping people out," Deborah cursed, leaning over to help.

Inside, three striped spheres nestled in a box.

"Juggling balls?" Katy questioned.

Deborah's bracelets jangled as she moved a hand through her hair. "They help relieve stress. Dave was given some when he was in a place like this. Apparently, they were a godsend."

"Dave was in rehab?" Katy questioned. She pictured a confident, energetic man who ran a retail business.

"He had a break down too," Deborah added.

"What happened?"

"Pressure, stress. One minute, he remembers things being fine and the next it was like his world collapsed."

Katy took out a ball and squeezed it. It was soft. She guessed there were beans inside the ball.

"They are from the new shop," Deborah said.

Katy squeezed the ball again. She felt a tear well in an eye and roll down a cheek. When she started shaking, Deborah - who was crying too - held her.

"How are Mum and Dad taking it?" Katy asked afterwards, drying her eyes with a tissue.

"Do you want the truth or a sugar-coated lie?"

"The truth please."

"They are worried sick. They blame Richard of course. They say this wouldn't have happened if he hadn't started digging up the past. And now he has run off to Spain! He's probably lounging on a beach on the Costa del Sol."

"He's not on the coast," Katy corrected. "He's in Granada. He's got a job, a flat and a girlfriend."

"You're joking?"

"Not at all. That's what he said in his latest email."

"What's her name?"

"I don't know. I don't want to know either. And I don't blame him. I wasn't much fun to be with."

"He abandoned you Katy. You know what you should do?"

Katy shook her head. "What should I do?"

"Get a divorce and ruin the bastard."

After Deborah left, Katy remained on the edge of the bed. She still had the juggling ball in her hand.

"First, I'd better get better," she thought out loud.

10
37 Acacia Street (Revisited)

Richard was not lounging on a beach. He was lounging in bed though. He and Fiona had just made love. Now they were sitting up, drinking English breakfast tea.

"How are the classes going in X?" Fiona asked.

Richard groaned. "Do we have to talk about school?"

"I'd like to know."

Richard leaned his head against the bed stead and looked up at the ceiling. "Badly," he replied. "It's been a real struggle so far."

"Isn't there anyone whose willing to learn?"

A shy girl called Nuria came to mind.

"One good apple is all you need," Fiona added.

Richard shrugged. He really didn't want to think about X. He was just happy sitting in bed beside Fiona. She blew on her tea. "Leonardo and I got a letter from Victor this morning," she said. "He's now living in a community somewhere. Workin' the land. Says he's happy."

"That's great news. Is he planning to return to Granada?"

She shook her head. "I don't think so. Well, not yet."

Later, while changing, Fiona said: "Looking forward to seeing you at the drinks party this Friday."

Richard frowned. "Do you really expect me to show up?"

"We'd be offended if you didn't."

"We?"

Fiona smiled. "I am still married, Richard. Like you."

"I might not be for much longer," Richard replied. "I've told Katy that I am seeing someone."

"Did you say it was me."

"No, I think she might flip again if she knew that."

"Most probably," Fiona said. "Is she furious?"

"No, I think she might even be relieved."

But he was surprised at how indifferent he was feeling. He had tried to summon up the old memories of Edinburgh: long, lazy afternoons spent in pubs. Visits to galleries and cinemas. Walks over hills and across windswept beaches. They had been happy back then. And years later, when they had got back together in London and were married – when Victor wasn't mentioned, supposedly forgotten - they were happy again for a while. But it hadn't lasted long.

*

On Friday evening, Richard did go to 37 Acacia street. The exterior of the house was bare compared to summer: the creepers and climbers that decorated its walls had lost their flowers. Some pot plants on a window ledge had withered. The patio table and chairs looked lonely. And the bicycle was no longer leaning against a wall.

Richard rang the bell. Fiona appeared holding a glass of wine. She looked beautiful in a long dress. She pressed a buzzer and Richard opened the gate. He walked across the patio to the front door. "Welcome," she said giving him a quick kiss and squeezing his arm.

Inside the house, it was warm. Most of the other guests had arrived and were gathered in the sitting room. Leonardo was at the centre of things, chatting with friends. He looked relaxed, wearing an open neck shirt, cream slacks and brown loafers. There was a cigar in his right hand. Fiona gave Richard a glass of wine. “I’ll be over in a moment,” she said.

Richard joined the huddle of Newman English school staff and their partners: Mike and Susie, Ray Elfrick and his wife (Richard couldn’t remember her name), Tanya West and her husband, José Pablo, who had a bristling moustache and was talking about the Easter processions.

“My favourite brotherhood is *La Fervorosa Hermandad de Nazarenos y Cofradía de Penitencia del Santísimo Cristo de la Buena Muerte y Nuestra Señora del Amor y del Trao*,” he said proudly.

“The who?” Mike asked.

Everyone laughed.

“If he was English,” Tanya said. “He’d be a train spotter.”

Richard looked at a framed photograph of Victor on a side table. In the photograph, Victor was wearing a v neck jersey over a white shirt and tie. He seemed to be staring right back. Richard wondered when the photograph had been taken. Perhaps two years ago, he thought

Later, he excused himself. And went to the loo. But instead of returning to the party, he walked quietly up the stairs. Creeping down the passage. He peered into a large bedroom. Fiona and Leonardo’s, he guessed looking at the double bed, and quickly moved on.

Victor’s room was at the end. The single bed was made, the furniture wiped clean. About a dozen photos of Victor nestled on a chest of drawers: a baby in the arms of Fiona, a toddler, a schoolboy, playing football, lying on a beach, in front of the Eiffel Tower with classmates.

Richard walked over to the desk. The letter Fiona had mentioned earlier in the week was on it. He picked it up:

Dear Mum and Dad, I just wanted you to know that I am well. In fact, I have never been better. I am living in a community in the mountains. We work the land and keep livestock. We grow crops, fruit and vegetables. It is hard but I am learning a lot. More than I did than when I was at school. Love Victor.

While Richard was reading the letter, Leonardo appeared in the doorway. The Spaniard stood there for a moment. Then he tapped the bedside table so Richard jumped. Both men stared at each other.

"He must be a fine lad," Richard said putting the letter down.

"He *was* a fine lad," Leonardo replied. "Now get out of my house."

11
Changing the World

I wish Mendez and his so-called friends would leave, Victor thought, one evening in the clearing where a fire blazed. He was sitting next to Gunne, a Norwegian, tucking into a chicken leg. They don't help with any of the chores. They don't tend the vegetable plots or help look after the animals. They just loaf around all day, digging into the rations that were supposed to last the whole winter.

Victor knew that they were shooting up too. Heroin. That would explain the mood swings, he thought, as he watched the group of men. The five of them, including Mendez, standing around the fire in the clearing. Two were wearing hoodies. Mean-looking bastards, he thought while listening to what the group were saying:

"Why are you really here *hermano*?" Arsenio was asking.

"You know I'm a wanted man so I have to hide away," Mendez replied. He took a couple of drags on a joint and passed it over to Estrella but she shook her head. Victor was pleased. He didn't like her smoking, it made her behave in a strange way. Like someone or something else was controlling her mind.

"But you aren't a wanted man any more," Arsenio said. "That policeman you shot has recovered. You're in the clear."

"Really? I don't think so. That couldn't be so easily forgotten."

"The police have other things on their minds. Now you can return to the city again."

"Well, I'll think about it," Mendez said. "If I stay here any longer, I'll go crazy."

"I would too," Arsenio nodded, looking around. "Hanging out with this bunch of frightened rabbits. How are you going to change the world if you burrow here?"

Victor put down his chicken. At the same time, Plácido rested a hand on his arm. Gunne now stood up. Gunne was from Trondheim. He was the oldest resident of Puerto Lobo. He was an impressive figure too sporting a thick beard and matching Arsenio in size. "Trying to change the world is no easy matter," he said in a gruff voice. "Your violent demonstrations don't do any good. Shooting policemen, picking fights, smashing up cashpoint machines, burning cars, that shit doesn't change anything. It just does harm."

And Gunne knew about fighting the system. Before coming to Puerto Lobo, he had worked as a front line activist for Greenpeace. He had helped stop a global company's illegal logging operation in Tasmania, he had disrupted whaling in Japan and helped close down a solar panel factory, which was polluting a river, in Brazil. He had also served two stretches in prison. Now he was married with two kids. His wife, Kristina, who was with him now, was eight months pregnant.

Arsenio shook his head: "You are mistaken Gunne. Revolution is the only way to liberate the state from corruption and vice."

The others nodded but Gunne just laughed. It was a loud laugh. "You lot have been brainwashed by your own propaganda," he said.

Arsenio glared at Gunne. "I don't know about you guys," he said crunching up his can of beer and throwing it across the clearing. "But I haven't come here to get insulted by some *cabron* Viking."

Mendez nodded and kicked his plate of food towards the fire. "I think this place stinks," he said.

"Then leave," Victor said. He was standing too. "And good riddance."

"Not before we wreck this place," Mendez replied, glaring at Victor.

"Over my dead body," Gunne said.

"As you wish," Arsenio then said.

Arsenio and Gunne now faced each other, moving in a circle in the clearing, like huge crabs, each eyeing his opponent. But it wasn't a fair fight because Arsenio produced a knife and lunged. Then another man charged forward and bulldozed into Gunne. Gunne fell to the floor and Arsenio kicked him in the stomach. Kristina started screaming. But Arsenio just kicked Gunne again.

That was when Plácido entered the fray. He kicked Arsenio on the wrist with his left foot so the knife fell to the floor. Then he floored Arsenio with his fist. The man who had bulldozed into Gunne, lunged at Plácido. So Plácido kicked him in the ribs with his right foot. "Get Kristina and the kids out of here," he shouted to Victor, while hopping around, looking this way and that, like a one-armed Bruce Lee in Enter the Dragon, as two other men advanced.

Victor began guiding Kristina and the kids away. But Mendez blocked the way. He punched Victor in the face. It hurt like hell. Victor stood, bent over, holding his nose, trying to stall the flow of blood.

By then Gunne, was up again. With Kristina, Estrella and the kids watching, he grabbed Mendez and knocked him to the floor. After that, the fight turned really messy. But Plácido and Gunne drove Arsenio and the other anarchists out of the camp.

*

"Where did you learn to fight like that?" Victor asked Plácido some time later, sitting on a fallen trunk in the clearing, his nose bloody and swollen, distorting his breathing and making his voice sound as if it came from far away.

"The army," Plácido replied.

"You were in the army?"

"I spent four years in the Legion."

Victor was surprised. He couldn't imagine Plácido being in the armed forces. Let alone the Spanish Legion. He was normally such a relaxed, peaceful man.

"Did you see any action?" Victor asked.

"A little," Plácido replied. "In Afghanistan."

"Is that where you lost your arm?"

The Asturian shook his head. "I lost the arm in a car crash near my home town."

"What happened?"

"I was drunk driving. Lost control of my vehicle while going round a bend. Smashed into the car coming the other way. A passenger in that other vehicle was killed, the driver was injured for life. They were an old couple, living peacefully in the town where I grew up."

Victor didn't know what to say. Then Estrella appeared across the clearing. She stood alone outside her cabin, the wind tugging at her hair. Mendez had ransacked it. And smashed her guitar as a leaving present. It lay in pieces at her feet.

12
Art Therapy

Katy was in the Gregory Lister Art room of the Wellhouse. Standing at a work table. Wearing a green apron like the other patients. She was listening to Hans Teuling saying: "Today, we're going to assemble and paint a plywood stationary holder. It's easy. A piece of cake, as the English say."

Katy smiled. Next to her, John cursed under his breath. Then he started tapping the table with his fingers. Katy tried to ignore the rock musician. She listened to Hans explain the process of construction. It is the sort of thing a seven-year-old could do, she thought, looking down at the box in front of her.

"Any questions?" Hans asked when he was through.

Professor MacGregor raised his hand.

"Yes Mark?" Hans said.

"Shouldn't we paint the item first?" he wheezed.

Katy knew the professor had been the head of a prestigious university Mathematics department. Now, he was barely able to tie up his own shoelaces.

"I can't verify this but if you assemble first," the professor continued. "Then surely the subsequent operation of applying paint will be greatly hindered. However, if you paint first, you need to be certain that you are undertaking your task on the correct side. You could be painting an interior when you are, in actual fact, working on an exterior flank. I think that, under the circumstances..." He faltered now, losing the thread of his own argument.

"Just do what it says on the instructions man!" John suddenly bellowed.

Katy jumped. So did Emily who was standing on her right.

"You just do as you wish Mark," Hans said to the professor. Then he went over and had a word with John.

Five minutes later, Katy was arranging the pieces of her kit on the surface of the table. She was concentrating hard; her tongue poking out of her mouth. She slowly fitted the sides to the base. Following the instructions. Careful with the glue. It suddenly occurred to her that she felt OK. Momentarily free from anxiety. It was as if she had been released from a cell. She wondered if it was because she had told herself that it was time to change her life. Or is it because you are taking all your pills?

"Have you got another kit mate?" John now shouted out to Hans. "I've ballsed up mine."

"That's not so bad John," Hans said.

John stared down at the gluey eyesore he had produced. "What are you talking about? It's a pile of shite."

"Well, we don't have any spare."

John sighed. "OK. But I ain't gonna find no buyer down Portobello."

"The Tate Modern might accept it love," a woman said. Her name was Lindsey Walsh and her face was a peculiar shade of grey.

"You're funny Lindsey," John said. "You know that."

"I try," Lindsey replied with a smile that revealed a rotten set of teeth. "I try."

Another few minutes ticked by. Katy finished assembling. Then she painted her kit. Meanwhile, Emily was struggling to connect two pieces together.

"Why don't you give Emily a hand love, now your done?" John suggested.

Katy kept her eyes front, refusing to acknowledge his presence. John repeated his question. Katy picked up the paint brush again. And pretended to touch up her piece. "Why don't you mind your own business?" she replied.

13
Mike

Not long after being kicked out of the party by Leonardo, Richard went to see Fiona's brother, Mike. Mike lived in a small flat in the Albaycin, the old Islamic quarter of Granada, within its maze of narrow streets where ivy, jasmine and bouganvillaea stretched their tendrils over high walls.

Behind these walls, luxurious villas were hidden. Their doorways decorated by onion shaped arches and hieroglyphics. Mike's small flat was next to one of the *miradors*. He shared it with Susie and a wolfhound called Boabdil. "I can't offer you any booze mate, so how about tea?" he told Richard in a cubby-hole kitchen. So they sat on the terrace with their mugs, gazing across the valley at the Alhambra. The Sierra Nevada its backdrop.

"I never get tired of this view," Mike sighed while stroking Boabdil who had curled up at his feet. They talked about other breath-taking views, Richard remembering a sea view from a cottage he and Katy had once rented in Wales.

"Sea views frighten the life out of me," Mike said. "I once tried to drive off Beachy Head."

"You're joking, right?" Richard replied.

"Not at all. When Eileen, my ex-wife became pregnant, she gave me an ultimatum; a family or booze."

"And you chose the booze?" Richard said.

"Right," Mike replied.

He scratched his neck. Then he continued: "So Eileen kicked me out. Then I lost my job teaching at a school in Eastbourne. After that, I lost my mind. I spent entire days in pubs. Until I was kicked out at closing time. I would stumble along the streets trying to find my van. In the morning, I would wake up not knowing how I had got there. Then I would get up and start all over again."

"One day, I drove the van to Beachy Head. I just sat there, in a car park, staring through the windscreen. I knew that if I lowered the hand brake, the car would roll forward, over the edge of the cliff and into the sea. All I had to do was lower that lever and my pain would be over. I couldn't bring myself to do it though. I was too much of a coward."

"Coward?"

"It takes guts to top yourself."

"But it's a cop out too, isn't it?" Richard argued. "I reckon it takes more guts to keep going."

Mike thought about that. "Perhaps. Anyway, afterwards, I decided that if I couldn't top myself, I might as well sort myself out. So that's what I did. Three months later, I was clean."

"What about Eileen?"

"When I rang her, she said she didn't want anything to do with me and she didn't want me coming to see our baby daughter either. She was making a new life for herself and the kid. She was frightened that I would screw it up. So I left the UK and came here. It was for the best."

"Don't you have any contact with your daughter?"
"I have never seen her," Mike replied.
"I only saw my son once," Richard said.
"Oh? I didn't know you were a father," Mike said.
"Hasn't Fiona told you?"
"No," Mike said.
Richard offered a weary smile. "It's a long story."
Mike leaned back in his chair and said: "I'm all ears."

14
Delivery

Victor carried a large pan through the snow on the path that led to the cabin of the Norwegian family. The cabin was situated on one of the terraces above the clearing and a layer of snow covered its roof and terrace and the vegetable plot that surrounded it.

After kicking the snow off his boots, he knocked on the cabin door. Gunne opened it and let him in. In the sitting room, Alf and Knut, the boys, were sitting in front of a roaring fire. There was a kitchen to one side of the room with a rustic table where the family ate.

It was here that the parents tutored the children with the help of other members of the community. Victor helped them with maths, English and science, and Estrella gave music lessons. But at this moment, no one in the family was thinking about class because Kristina, Gunne's wife, was about to give birth.

Victor rested the pan on the table. Then he touched his face with the sleeve of his jersey. Grimacing slightly when he brushed his nose which was still out of shape from Mendez's blow.

Gunne led Victor into the main bedroom where Kristina was lying down, blowing air from round cheeks like a puffer fish.

Plácido was counting the contractions. Estrella was perched on the edge of the bed, hair tied into a pony tail, mopping the Norwegian woman's large brow with a damp cloth.

"Is the birth imminent?" Gunne asked Plácido.

"Pretty close. I'll need you to deliver. I would but it's difficult with one arm."

Gunne, whose voice was gruff and who towered over everyone else in the cabin, shook his head. "No way. I'll faint."

Both of them turned to Estrella.

"I get really squeamish too," she said.

So everyone looked at Victor.

"Me?" he whispered.

*

"Push!" Victor urged. He was kneeling down at the end of the bed, his eyes tightly closed. His hands squeezed between Kristina's legs, feeling a gelatinous membrane. "Push!" he repeated.

Kristina bared her teeth. When she screamed, Victor felt the top of a tiny cranium through warm blood. "One last time!" he shouted. She screamed again. A matt of black hair was visible. Then the sticky infant slipped out, into Victor's arms. Victor, blood soaked, held up the baby and Plácido quickly cut the umbilical cord. He told Victor to tie a knot. "Now smack her on the butt," Plácido said.

Afterwards, Estrella washed and dried the baby. Victor took took off his bloody shirt, threw it in the bin and put on his jersey. "Congratulations!" Plácido said to Gunne who had chosen to wait outside the room with his boys. "You have a girl." Gunne and the boys came inside. Estrella handed Gunne the child. Then she stood by Victor. They watched in silence as Gunne showed the infant to her brothers. Then the Norwegian gave her back to Kristina. She took the child in her arms, smiled and fell asleep from exhaustion.

Later, Victor and Estrella stood together in the clearing and looked up at the stars. It was a clear, cold night. The Milky Way, a subtle brush stroke in the sky. "I'd like to live here forever," Estrella said leaning her head against Victor's shoulder.

"Me too," he replied. He felt elated. In fact, he couldn't remember ever feeling so happy.

"But good things always come to an end," Estrella added.

"They don't have to."

"They always do."

Victor thought of Mendez who hadn't been seen since leaving Puerto Lobo. "Well, maybe they won't this time."

Estrella smiled and snuggled closer against him. Then he gazed into her large brown eyes and they kissed.

Afterwards, they went to her cabin. Inside, it was warm from read coals smouldering in a burner. She lit two candles and a stick of incense. Then they lay down together on the bed. Estrella pressed her warm body against his. She slipped her hand between his jeans and enclosed her fingers around his penis. He groaned with pleasure. Then they undressed and crawled under the blankets. They kissed some more.

"Why don't you take off your top?" he asked but she didn't reply. Instead, she ran her finger tips down his body. He shivered, feeling ripples of delight. Then he climbed on top and she guided him into her.

15
The Niagra Falls

~~Breakfast~~
~~Yoga session~~
~~Thank you letter to Katy and Dave~~
Juggle
Positive Thinking session
Lunch
Rest
Meditation session – 3 o'clock
Walk
Tea
Juggle
Diary
Supper
Shower
Bed

Katy stood with her feet slightly apart in the centre of the room. When she threw the juggling ball up, it curved through the air and landed in her other hand. Then she repeated the movement. Afterwards, she juggled two balls. Then she tried three. But she kept on dropping them. In frustration, she hurled the balls angrily against the wall. One of them hit her walking stick which fell on the carpet. It remained there when she left the room. She was clutching her 'thank you' letter, instead.

Later, Katy went to the canteen. And sat down at an empty table. Emily entered the room. Normally, Emily was accompanied by a nurse at meal times. But not today, Katy thought, which meant Emily was making progress in her struggle against bulimia.

When Emily sat down at the table, Katy cringed. Then she forced a smile. Emily smiled too. Katy prodded a lettuce leaf and put it in her mouth.

"What's that like?" Emily asked.

Katy crunched the lettuce. "Pretty tasteless," she replied.

"That's because it comes from Spain."

Katy thought of Richard. "Does it?"

Emily nodded. "It's from the Almeria region."

"Oh?"

"Almeria means Mirror to the Sea."

Katy leaned forward. "Have you been there?"

"Yes, a long time ago. It's like a desert. Sucked dry."

Emily peeled a banana and then began cutting it, in extremely thin slices with a knife. She carefully laid the slices on the creamy surface of yoghurt in a bowl.

"That's very beautiful," Katy said.

"Thank you."

"And I'm sure it'll taste very good."

"Do you think so?"

Katy nodded. "Go on. Try some."

Emily stared at the bowl. Then she picked up a spoon and slowly dipped it into the yoghurt. When she put the spoon into her mouth, the yoghurt dribbled down her chin. Katy felt repulsion. And wanted to leave. Instead, she handed Emily a tissue.

When Katy finished her meal and was about to leave the canteen, Emily asked if she could stay a while.

"OK," Katy said. "But on one condition."

"What?"

"You finish up."

So Emily slowly ate her food. Every once in a while, Katy handed the skinny woman a fresh tissue. To curb the Niagra Falls, she thought.

16
Nativity Scene

"I think Leonardo suspects something," Fiona said to Richard in café bar Luna in the Realejo. It was the cosy establishment, hidden down a side street, they often frequented.

"Why do you think that?"

"He keeps asking me about you. And he wanted to know where I was going tonight. We can't go on like this."

"Perhaps we should talk to him then."

Fiona's eyes widened. "Are you serious?"

Richard nodded. "Why not?"

"He would freak out."

"Why? He's been seeing other women."

"In his eyes, that's different. Anyway, I meant that *I* can't go on like this."

Fiona took a swig of wine. "It's nothing to do with you," she explained. "Quite the opposite in fact. You've kept me going. Everything else in my life has gone pear shaped: Victor hasn't come home, Leonardo and I argue constantly, the school is a never-ending struggle." She shook her head. "I guess I'm burned out. I need a change. I need to get away."

Richard studied Fiona's face. "Where would you go?"

Fiona shrugged. "I don't know. Madrid probably. I have friends and contacts there."

Richard nodded.

"You don't seem surprised," Fiona said.

"Well, you're right. We can't go on like this forever."

He took a letter from his jacket pocket and passed it to Fiona. It was from his father:

Richard,

It has come to my ears that Katy is filing for divorce. I can understand why. You promised to love and cherish her. To look after her in sickness and health. To be faithful to her. Yet it appears you have done the exact opposite. Not only have you run away from an invalid, but you are playing away (if what I hear is true). It's your duty to return. Not just to your wife but to the business you have neglected. If you don't, I would strongly consider changing the content of my will and this won't be to your benefit.

Yours sincerely,

Father

After Fiona had read it, they drank for a moment in silence. "As you can see, I need to straighten things out too," Richard said.

"Will you come back?"

"Of course."

After a couple more drinks, they left the café bar and walked down the hill towards Richard's flat together. The Christmas lights were up. Not far away, Silent Night was being sung.

"I wish I could drive you to Malaga tomorrow," Fiona said.

"I do too," Richard replied.

"But it's impossible."

"I know."

They stopped and faced each other. He leaned forward and they kissed.

In the hallway of the block of flats, they kissed again. Richard then fumbled for the light switch. But someone emerged from the darkness and punched Richard in the face. Then in the stomach. Richard grunted and fell to the floor. Fiona screamed.

It was Leonardo. He stood stone-faced yet bristling over Richard who had curled up on the floor. A door opened on the floor above and the sound of feet could be heard hurrying down the stairs. Leonardo grabbed Fiona and dragged her outside. When the door was slammed shut, loose plaster fell from the ceiling. Like soggy confetti thrown at the end of a doomed wedding.

*

"¡Que bestia! ¡Que bestia!" Pilar, Gonzalo's wife, tutted while nursing Richard's cuts and bruises. His head pounded and his ears were ringing They were sitting at a table in the flat Pilar and Gonzalo owned. Lights twinkled on a Christmas tree in a corner. On a shelf, there was a Nativity scene; Joseph and Mary standing either side of the baby Jesus in the stable. While the three kings and the shepherds waited patiently outside.

Gonzalo poured some DYC whisky into a glass. "The police are on the way to your lady friend's house," he said handing the glass to Richard.

"Good," Richard replied. Then he downed the whisky and felt its kick.

"I hope they grab that beast of a man," Pilar added. "He should be locked away."

"I provoked him," Richard said. "After all, I've been sleeping with his woman."

Pilar paused. "What did you say *hombre*?" Her tone was accusing. Normally, if she met Richard on the stairs or on the street, she ran quickly past with her head bowed. But now she stood erect and pushed out her ample chest.

"I've been sleeping with his woman," Richard repeated.

"So that was the husband of *la mujer con solamente una bota?"* Pilar whispered.

Richard nodded; the woman with one boot! So Pilar had spied Fiona's hurried exit back in October.

"*La mujer con solamente una bota*," Gonzalo said. "I've been hearing about her." Then he frowned. "But what became of the other boot?"

"It was returned," Richard said.

Gonzalo picked up the DYC whisky bottle. "Ah," he said pouring Richard another shot.

Richard downed the second shot, The whisky burned his throat and ran wild in his stomach. He exhaled and wiped his mouth with the back of a hand. Pilar watched him in silence. The fingers on her right hand slowly closing to form a fist. "So that was her poor husband," she said. "You'll have to ask the Lord for forgiveness." Gonzalo rested his hand on Pilar's shoulder to calm her.

Richard assented. And tried to focus on the Nativity scene. But, the whisky made his eyes stream with tears. The tears blurred the sombre faces of the shepherds and three wise men standing outside the stable. And they blurred Mary and Joseph and the baby Jesus who had come down to save the world.

17
Damaged

Victor hammered the fence post into the ground with a sledge hammer. Then, using a spade, he filled the base with loose soil. He paused and took a swig of water from a bottle. Wiping some sweat from his brow, watching Plácido and Gunne further down the slope. Enjoying the warmth of the sun on a winter's day, the sensation of peace.

During the night, gale force winds had torn through the valley. Causing the fence to come down and some pigs to flee. Miraculously, other damage was minimal: only a few of the older trees in the orchards had been blown over. Most importantly, no one was harmed. Gunne had told him that Astrid, the baby Victor had delivered, slept peacefully through the entire storm.

Victor thought about Estrella. They had lain in his bed, curled up in each others arms. Listening to the howling wind. I hope there is another gale tonight, he thought with a smile. Or better still a blizzard! Or lightning and thunder! Bring it on mother nature. As long as we are together. He knew he was in love with her.

What is it about her, he wondered. Last night, I felt so close to her yet sometimes she is like a stranger. Why can she be so nasty? Just the other day, she locked herself in her cabin and refused to come out. And on another occasion, she disappeared without a word. Why? He wondered. Then another part of him said not to worry. That everyone is different. Let her run free. You don't want to turn into a Mendez and rule over Estrella like a tyrant.

A short time later, while Victor was hammering another post home, Estrella came down the path. When she saw Victor, she stopped in her tracks. And crouched down like a hunted animal. She remained in that position for five or six seconds. Then she moved hurriedly on.

Later, Kristina came by. She looked flustered. Although Astrid was sound asleep in a sling on her back.

"What's up?" Victor asked.

"Have you seen Estrella?"

"No."

"Well, she has missed her class."

The first thing Victor did, on returning to the camp, was go to Estrella's cabin. The door was open so he called out her name. But there was no reply. Inside the cabin, the bed was unmade and clothes littered the floor. A glass star, a Christmas decoration, lay in pieces on the floor. Victor picked the pieces up, trying to work out what had happened.

There was a vinegary smell in the bathroom. And a table spoon in the sink. Its base was burned. He touched the bowl of the spoon and licked the tip of his finger. Is that what I think it is? he wondered with a grimace. There was a wash bag under the sink. Inside this, Victor found a hypodermic needle, some cigarette filters, a cord and a bag of heroin.

*

“I’ve been searching all over for you,” he said when he eventually found her. She was lying in a hammock, staring up at the sky.

“Have you?” she replied, turning her head slightly and smiling. There was a glazed look in her eyes.

“You missed your class. Kristina was worried.”

She returned her gaze to the sky. “Oh,” she said as if it was nothing to do with her.

Victor leaned over and lifted her left arm. Then he pushed back the sleeve of her jersey. The main line vein of her left forearm was punctured in various places. There were three other, older marks too. Always hidden from view, he thought. “Did you buy it down in the town?” he asked angry now.

She nodded.

“Who from?”

She looked at him. She was smiling. It was a cruel smile. She said: “Mendez.”

*

That evening, as the sun dropped behind the hills, Estrella perched on the edge of the bed in her cabin and put her head in her hands. The rims of her eyes were red.

“Where’s my dope?” she asked Victor.

“I chucked it on the fire.”

“You what?”

“I burned it.”

Estrella glared at Victor. He could see the anger inside her rise. “How about some soup?” he asked holding up a thermos flask.

Victor unscrewed the top of the flask. Then he poured some of the soup into it and placed it on the table. Estrella didn’t touch the cup. She remained on the bed with her elbows on her knees and her chin resting in the palms of her hands. "Why don't you try some?" Victor asked.

"I am not fucking hungry."

"Suit yourself. Shall I light the wood burner? It's getting cold."

"I'll do it," she quickly said.

"It's no problem, I can..."

"Just fuck off," she interrupted.

He stood for a moment looking at her.

"Go away," she repeated.

Victor turned and made his way to the door. As he was leaving, she picked up the cup and threw it. The soup flew through the air. The cup just missed Victor's head. And bounced off the wall.

18
Wild Horses

"How was the walk?" Gail, the receptionist at the Wellhouse, asked while Katy wiped her feet on the doormat.

"Hard work," Katy replied, out of breath. But she felt pretty good. Her cheeks flushed. She knew that her health was improving: she was feeling more energetic and she had lost weight. "I would not have been able to do that walk a month ago," she said.

"Well, you are making really good progress," Gail said. Katy thanked Gail. Then she walked down the corridor towards her room. At the end of the passage, she paused. Someone was playing the piano. Well, trying to, she thought.

In the music room, John was hunched over the Cavendish piano. The back of his shirt drenched in sweat. Katy watched and cringed. The rock star was trying to play the Rolling Stones' Wild Horses. She knew the song well having once played it in a school concert. But this version was painful to the ear. And the stench of body odour. Repulsive.

John suddenly slammed the piano lid down with a bang. "I can't fucking do it," he swore to the wall. Katy remained by the door. She wanted to creep away but she found she couldn't bring herself to.

"It starts on a B minor," she heard herself say instead.

John turned around. And glared at her. "What the hell are you doing? Spying on me?" he began angrily.

"It's B,B,D,F," she interrupted moving forward. "May I?"

Without waiting for a reply, she sat down beside him on the bench and raised the piano lid again. Then she rested her fingers on the keys.

At first, she fumbled to find the right notes. Then the song came back to her. She repeated the part John was having trouble with. "Now you try," she said.

His fat fingers trembled as he played and messed up again.

"It's la-La-la," she corrected taking a clammy hand and guiding it over the keys. He faulted. The next go, he got it. And then he did it again. Better. He began to sing. His voice was rough around the edges but it was strong. When he finished, he carefully closed the lid and sat facing front, in silence. A tear rolled down his face.

John told Katy his story. Of drugs and rock n' roll.

"Not much sex though," he admitted. "I couldn't get it up half the time."

"Didn't your wife know?"

"What? That I couldn't get it up?"

Katy rolled her eyes.

"She never knew," he said. "I only behaved badly on tour. At home, I was the model husband until one night I was high and paranoid and I thought my wife was cheating on me. It didn't seem to matter that I was cheating on her. I flipped. I smashed the TV and wrecked the sitting room. She rang the police. It took three of them to pin me down and then a doctor was called. He administered a tranq." Katy shivered. She remembered hearing about it on the news. "My stomach got pumped in a hospital," John added. "Then I was transferred to this hole."

"Well, that's all over now," Katy said turning and facing him. "We have to try and forget the past and concentrate on the present."

John closed the piano lid. "So I'm told. But it's easier said than done."

"Tell me about it," Katy said.

19
Christmas Eve

The morning after being beaten up by Leonardo, Richard's face was bruised. His body sore. But he was more worried about Fiona. As she didn't answer her phone, he dressed and staggered out the door. On the stairs, Gonzalo was putting a Christmas wreath on his door. "How are you feeling today *hombre*?" the hairdresser asked.

"Like shit," Richard replied continuing down the stairs and stumbling out into another bright day.

On 37 Acacia street, the window shutters were down. The car was gone. He rang the doorbell and stood bracing himself against a cold wind. No reply. He rang Fiona's mobile number again. Nothing. He rang Leonardo's mobile. Nothing. So he turned and walked away.

Instead of going home he wandered into the centre of town. Occasionally, he would stop and gaze through a shop window. At displays festive with Christmas figures, glitter and tinsel. He was confused. Unsure of which way to go. Like a runaway who has come to the end of the line.

Eventually, he came to an empty square. Crumbling flats with rusty balconies, looked solemnly down upon it. He sat on a bench. Some sparrows landed and pecked at crumbs on the ground. A breeze rustled the dead leaves of a tree. He felt as if he had been in this place before. But of course I have, he thought. It had been summer and he had come here to read a book. He remembered watching a tramp asleep where he was sitting now.

The phone rang. He picked up.

"How's it going?" a voice asked. It was Mike.

Richard hesitated. "Not well."

"Fiona told me about last night. I gather you took a bit of a beating. Are you OK?"

"Yes. How is she? I've tried to call."

"She's a little shaken but otherwise fine. She's flown the nest. She has left Leonardo. Even as we speak, she's on her way to a friend's house in Madrid. She needs to think things over."

"Yes," Richard said. "She does."

"What are you doing tonight?" Mike asked.

"Tonight?"

"Ding dong. It's Christmas Eve."

Richard glanced at his watch. "I am supposed to be flying to the UK but I just can't face it."

"We're having a small party here. Why don't you come on over? And drown your sorrows instead."

So that night, Richard tore up his boarding pass, bought some booze and trudged through the dark, narrow streets of the Albaycin. A drunk Father Christmas lurched by on a moped. Then a laughing family bustled past. He caught a whiff of roasting meat. Then he heard music and laughter. Yet he felt separate from the warmth those sensations had to offer. Not like a guest to a party, he realised. More like a deserter, who is running from battle.

20
Shit Happens

Estrella fumbled for the switch in the darkness. When the bed side lamp was on, she lowered it to the ground and draped a towel over it to dim the brightness. Then she quietly changed. After that, she crept over to the chest of drawers. She opened three draws before finding the envelope. After looking inside, she folded the envelope and put it in the back pocket of her jeans.

Before leaving the cabin, she went back to the bed, bent down and kissed Victor. He murmured, rolling over in his sleep. Then she turned off the lamp and walked to the door. Outside, dawn was breaking. She wrapped her coat tight around her and crept down the path. Her warm breath cloudy. Her feet crunching over the frosty ground. Tears rolled down her cheek.

She entered her own cabin and picked up the two bags she had packed the previous night. Then she made her way down to the car park where a figure was waiting by a Jeep. It was Carlos Mendez.

"You're late," he said. "Did you get the cash?" She nodded and gave him the envelope. He counted the money. "Good," he said. Estrella remained standing for a moment. Studying the outline of the valley in the dawn light. Mendez opened the driver's side door. "Come on," he said gruffly.

*

Victor awoke long after Estrella had left Puerto Lobo. He wondered why the bedside lamp was on the floor. Then he wondered where Estrella had gone.

Since he had found the heroin, they had talked. Estrella promising Victor she wasn't addicted. That she only shot up once in a while. But that she would be clean from now on. Victor climbed out of bed. While he changed, he noticed the third drawer of the chest was open. So he walked over and looked inside.

Five minutes later, he walked down to Estrella's cabin. The door was open. When he looked inside, he saw that the cabin was empty.

"Have you guys seen Estrella?" he asked Plácido and Gunne later.

"Nope," Plácido replied.

"The Jeep has gone," Gunne said.

Victor looked through the trees, down to the car park. "So has Estrella and my savings. But she can't drive."

"Then Mendez must have come here."

Victor sat on a tree trunk on the edge of the clearing. Leaning forward, with the tips of his fingers pressing against his forehead. Not far away, Kristina was washing some clothes. The boys were playing. Astrid, the infant, was sleeping in a pram. And Gunne could be heard chopping some wood behind the cabin where the family lived.

Neither the presence of the Norwegian family nor the sun could cheer Victor up. He felt unbalanced. Empty. As if the ground had been whipped away from under his feet. It was like falling, he thought, and there was nothing to hold onto.

Plácido came over and sat down next to Victor. He took out his pouch of tobacco and rolled a cigarette with his one good hand. Then he lit up. Victor smelled the tobacco smoke. And thought of Leonardo and Fiona. He wondered how they were.

Plácido coughed. "Well," he said.
"Well what?" Victor asked.
"Well, shit happens," Plácido replied.
"*Si*," Victor said. "But you never see it coming."

21
Homeward Bound

"How are you feeling?" Doctor Kernowe asked Katy in consulting room 3, while polishing the lenses of his burgundy-rimmed glasses with a cloth. He had a checked shirt on, open at the collar. Katy studied his face. It was peppered with freckles. Without glasses, it looked alien, somehow naked.

"Better," she said. "I feel better now."

Doctor Kernowe put the glasses back on. Then he turned to his right and said: "What do you think Peter?"

Doctor Mann had been sitting in silence. As usual, he was dressed in a pale blue suit and wearing a tie. His blonde hair carefully combed and parted to one side. Katy had never heard Doctor Kernowe refer to Doctor Mann as Peter. In fact, she had never even considered the doctor might possess a Christian name.

For a moment, Peter Mann consulted the file. Then he looked up and stroked his chin. "Your progress has been excellent. The staff have also commented on the way you have been helping some of the other patients. So we think you are ready to go home Katy. But what do you think?" he asked. "Are you ready to leave this 'madhouse'?"

Katy barely remembered saying those words. And she wasn't sure if she *was* ready. She suddenly felt off balance. In the Wellhouse, life was ordered. She felt safe. Secure. Everything was done for her. Now, she would have to face the real world.

*

Katy looked around: at the bed, the chair, the walls, the juggling balls left on the desk. Through the window, the slender olive tree stood in the courtyard. Protected from the wind. Everything looked the same as when she had first entered that room. But she knew it was different.

She picked up her overnight bag and left the room. She walked silently down the passage, passing the music room and the Quiet Room. Thinking of John and Emily, Hans Teuling and nurse Jacks, Doctors Kernowe and Mann.

She went down the corridor that led to reception. On the walls, tinsel decorated the prints. She could make out her father at the end. He was standing in reception. His white hair shining under a neon tube of light.

Simon & Garfunkel could be heard on the radio in reception. Paul Simon softly singing about the repetitive aspects of touring, about feeling lonely, about cigarettes and magazines. Katy followed her father through the front door. Then outside into pale sunlight. She shivered, exhaling a cloud of cold air. And looked over the frosted cars parked in the driveway. Down the long avenue of oak trees. Away, into the distance. Homeward Bound.

SPRING

1
What Did You Get?

Richard was running along a steep path one morning in late March. His breath was laboured. His heart pumping fast. His face a blotchy red. Blood pulsing through the vessels in his head. Sweat clung to the T shirt on his back. Dust puffed up from under his feet, peppering his aching calves. But he refused to give up. Another step, he told himself. And another. The path gradually levelled out. And the going became easier again. He continued on. Lighter on his feet. Shaking his arms to loosen built-up tension.

A short time later, he came to a plateau. And stopped on the edge of a precipice. He put his hands on his hips. Catching his breath. Near by, mountain swifts planed on the thermals. Across the valley, the Sierra Nevada snoozed under the blue sky. The peaks, the crags, the gulleys: so clearly defined. The snow line mottled. Below, swathes of pine trees swept the foothills.

Richard smiled. It was a proper smile. The first for a while. When he had visited Katy in Twickenham, she refused to speak to him. Then James and Anne ordered him to leave their house. The following day, Katy's sister, Deborah, had visited Richard in Fulham and called him 'a cold and selfish bastard.' A number of friends had been a little more generous. But not by much.

The Brownlowe gallery was now closed. The last paintings in the in-house collection had been sold to pay for the astronomical Wellhouse bills. Richard had gone to Wiltshire and stayed a couple of days with his parents. But they continued their routines, almost ignoring his presence. So he left. To keep looking for my son, he had told them. Neither had wished him luck.

*

On return to his flat, Richard had a shower and changed. Afterwards, he lit a gas ring and put an aluminium coffee pot on it. The water soon boiling. The blood-like burning coffee squeezing its way upwards. The stove pot coughing and spluttering. Richard poured himself a *corto* into an *espresso* size mug and sat down. There was an old copy of El Ideal, a local newspaper, on the table. And a post card; the image on its face was Picasso's Dove of Peace. He read it again:

Dear Richard, Just to say that
all is well here in Madrid.
Thinking of you.
Love Fiona.
PS. Please keep an eye on Mike

Richard knew why Fiona had added the post script: Mike had recently split up with Susie. Mike taking things badly and leaving the flat in the Albaycin. Now, he lived in a van, parked on a street. Richard rang Mike's mobile. But there was no answer. I'll pop round soon, he told himself.

That afternoon, Richard took the bus to X in sombre mood. The empty streets, grey blocks of flats and widespread graffiti didn't lift his spirits. Nor did the imposing school building with its high walls lined with cut glass. In classroom 4, the bug-eyed students sprawled in their seats. He wondered why he had agreed to continue teaching them. When Leonardo won't have me near the NSE, he added to himself.

When he asked "How was your weekend?", the reply was a series of grunts. Then Raquel, a pretty girl, leaned provocatively forward at her desk.

"It was my birthday," she said.

"Congratulations," Richard replied. "So how old are you?"

"Sixteen."

"What did you get? Anything special?"

The girl, sitting at the next door desk, nudged Raquel, and they both giggled.

Richard drew a present on the board. "Can anyone remember what they got for their last birthday?"

No one could. So Richard turned his attention to a boy doodling in a note book: "Marcos?" Marcos shrugged without raising his eyes from the page. Behind Marcos, a girl with a shaven head was chewing gum. Her T shirt had a skull on the front. "What did you get Chelo?"

"I got tickets to a concert," she replied. She blew a bubble of gum and it popped.

"What about you then Dario?" Richard asked turning to another boy.

"I got Play Station."

"Pablo?"

"I got an ipad."

"Magda?"

"A Wii."

"Alba?"

"Nintendo and money."

"Tomás?"

"Call of Duty."

"Samu?"

"A lap top."

"Lydia?"

"A TV."

"Sonia?"

"I got 100 euros."

Not bad for a marginalised neighbourhood, Richard thought.

"What about you teacher?" someone then asked. "When was your birthday?"

"Back in December." Richard replied.

"What did you get?"

Richard scratched his head. December seemed long ago. I received a bill for thirty grand from the Wellhouse, he remembered. As well as a threatening letter from my father. It was around then that I got beaten up by Leonardo, followed by first aid from Pilar and whisky from Gonzalo.

"I got a scarf and money," he lied.

His gaze met the eyes of one student. Nuria, a quiet girl with mousy brown hair. She shook her head; it was as if she could see right through him.

2
Oh Ye Of Little Faith.

One fine, spring day, a green minibus skidded to a halt in the overgrown car park at Puerto Lobo. A side door opened and some children appeared. They stood in a huddle, looking around in wonder. Then some young teens got down from the van. They stretched and yawned.

After that, a woman appeared. The woman had long grey hair. She stood for a moment; her colourful dress wafting in a warm breeze. She smiled as she gazed at the log cabins on the green terraces, at the roaming animals, then down the valley to where the sky met the distant sea in a haze of blue.

Finally, an old man emerged from the back of the vehicle. He had white hair and was dressed in a grey suit and a pair of trainers. He seemed confused for a moment, but when the woman put an arm around him, he smiled.

Victor was standing beside Plácido, watching from a slope above: "Who are that lot?" he asked.

"Ángel and Elizabeth, the owners of this land," Plácido replied. "With the children from the city."

Ángel was Elizabeth's father. He had brought the land in the early 1980s. But he had never lived on it and it had gone wild. It was Elizabeth who had persuaded Ángel to let strangers come and go as long as the place was looked after, instead of leaving it to go to ruin. Now, they visited annually always bringing along a group of under privileged, city kids with them, for an educational holiday in a natural environment.

That night there was a party to welcome the newcomers. Plácido cooked a large paella over the fire in the clearing. Kristina prepared a salad, Astrid, the baby, in a sling on her back. Gunne and the kids were there too. Victor organised some games. There was singing and fireworks too.

Eventually, everyone went back to their cabins. In his, Victor lay in the darkness and thought about Estrella. It's strange, he thought. I really believed I had found love. But how can it have been? It was a lie and now I don't feel anything. Except lost again, like I did when I left home.

Victor had strange dreams that night. In one of them, he was sitting with his parents at the kitchen table in the house in Acacia street. A honey bee was circling the light. Then it changed course and started bumping against the window pane so Victor rose and walked over.

"Don't open the window," Leonardo warned.

"But the bee wants to go out," Victor said.

"Don't open the window," Leonardo repeated.

Victor didn't listen. He opened the window and another bee immediately flew in. Then another and another. They were everywhere. In his hair, stinging his face, crawling into his clothes and over his body. Fiona began screaming.

Victor opened his eyes. He lay, covered in sweat.

*

"You need to dig deeper this side," Ángel, dressed in his grey suit and trainers, said looking into a hole where Victor and Luis, a kid from the city, stood. Victor leaned on his spade, frowned and wiped his brow. Muddy water swilled around his boots. They were supposedly creating a series of 'natural' swimming pools but Victor wasn't enjoying the chore. Neither was Luis who cursed under his breath. Some of the others had already given up.

At the end of the day, Victor went to speak to Ángel and Elizabeth. Father and daughter were sitting on a grassy terrace under the shade of an almond tree.

"It's a mess," Victor said pointing at the series of holes.

"It's a mess all right," Ángel admitted.

"We need heavy machinery. One of those diggers."

"We don't need machinery," Ángel countered. "We need to work as a team. If we all work together, we'll get there. Rome wasn't built in a day, remember. And we're just creating some natural swimming pools on a hillside. That's nothing compared to building a city. It'll be worth the effort. You'll see."

"But..." Victor began.

"But nothing," Ángel replied.

Victor looked at Elizabeth for help. She lifted her cup and took a sip of tea. "Oh ye of little faith," she said with a wink.

3
Hope

Katy sat at the kitchen table in her parents' house in Twickenham. She was listening to a reporter interviewing a Chinese writer on Woman's Hour, Radio 4. Toblerone was snoozing on a stool beside her. Katy felt relaxed at that moment. But she knew the feeling wouldn't last forever. She had to take each day as it came. Lurking near by was the fear of falling back down into the mire of depression.

She studied a list of things to do:

~~Yoga.~~
~~Make the bed and clean the room.~~
Read – 20 minutes.
Go to the chemist.
Help Mum prepare lunch.
Wellhouse appointment: 3 pm.
Walk.
Read.

I'll never get through all of this reading, she thought, staring at a stack of books on the table beside her: Overcoming Mental Illness. Breaking Addiction. Organic Diet – The Road to Good

Digestion. Mindfulness. Gentle Yoga. Balzac and the Little Chinese Seamstress. Small Island. Mr. Lynch's Holiday. The previous day, she had binged in Waterstone's.

She picked up Balzac and the Little Chinese Seamstress. Remembering reading it at university. And loving every word. She began reading the first chapter. Then an email notification appeared on the screen of the lap top. It was from Richard. She didn't open the e mail. Instead, she pressed the delete button and continued reading the book.

After twenty minutes, she closed the book and left the house. She walked to the chemist to collect a new batch of pills. Enjoying the warmth spring was offering. Noticing the leaves, like tiny green sails, unfurling on the trees and bushes. Inhaling the aroma of the flowers.

Back at the house, she cooked a cottage pie with her mother's help. They ate it in the kitchen. James was out, playing golf. Anne talking about a new garden centre before turning the conversation to Katy's future.

"What are you going to do now?" she asked.

"I don't know," Katy replied.

"Perhaps you should get a job."

"Yes, but what?"

Anne looked at Katy. "After all your education? There must be something you can do!"

Afterwards, Katy made a cup of coffee and took it up to her room. She felt like she had been punched in the stomach. But Mum is right, she thought. There must be something I can do. She looked at a school photo on the wall. Then the shot of her wearing a mortar board and gown, holding her degree. "But what?" she repeated out loud.

At half past two, she removed the keys of the Triumph Spitfire from a rack in the hall. Richard had driven the Spitfire over from Fulham when he had been in the UK. She didn't regret refusing to see him. He had made the decision to live a separate life so it was over. There was nothing to talk about.

She drove through Twickenham with the top of the car down. Dressed in a coat and a hat. Enjoying the fresh air and the warmth of the sun on her face. On a dual carriageway, she passed fields of rape, wheat and barley. Oak and chestnut forests. She felt lost in a dream. Then she was heading down the Wellhouse avenue, the tyres crunching over gravel.

She parked facing the oppressive grey building. Inside, she chatted with Gail at reception. Then she sat down in one of the empty chairs outside consulting room 3 and waited for her appointment.

"We've got something to ask, haven't we Peter?" Doctor Kernowe said. Both doctors having expressed satisfaction with Katy's on-going progress.

"We have indeed," Doctor Mann concurred with a smile.

"Ask away," Katy replied.

"We wondered if you would like to work here as a trainee care worker?"

The suggestion took Katy by surprise. "But I'm not qualified," she replied.

"You don't need a qualification for a trainee position. There would just be some basic first aid training before you started. Isn't that right Peter?"

"That's correct," Doctor Mann said. "Applying is quite straightforward. You should talk to nurse Jacks about the position. She'll fill you in."

Could I really train to be a care worker, Katy wondered afterwards as she walked down the long corridor towards the Quiet Room. Then she remembered the cutting comment her mother had made at lunchtime and the sense of failure it had caused her. Now a potential opportunity had suddenly presented itself.

In the Quiet Room, nurse Jacks was sitting in a corner with a patient. Quentin was a skinny young man who had arrived a week back. He looked lost, staring out of the window at the fields beyond. Just like I did when I got here, Katy thought.

She waited a moment and then told nurse Jacks what the doctors had said. "But I don't know if I am suitable trainee material."

"You would be perfect," nurse Jacks said with a smile. "Afterwards, you might consider nursing as a profession."

"Me? A nurse?" Katy laughed. "You must be joking!"

Nurse Jacks looked her in the eye.

"Not at all."

4
The X Project

In X, class was over: Richard was reordering his text books while the students filed out of the room, chatting away. One student remained at her desk: Nuria, the quiet girl, with mousy brown hair. Now, she got up and walked over. Richard asked: "*¿Que pasa?* What's up?"

Nuria handed over a letter. It announced a competition organised by a global association of young entrepreneurs based in California. The association wanted innovative projects, that would help a local community. Entrants needed to write a project proposal in English. The winner would get fifty thousand US dollars.

"Do you want to enter?" Richard asked.

Nuria nodded.

"Have you got anything in mind?"

"I want to start the X project," Nuria said.

Richard pulled up a chair from another table so Nuria could sit down. "Tell me about it," he said.

"The idea is basic," Nuria explained. "When students leave the institute here in X, they get trained up in some area and learn a skill. Maybe IT, plumbing, mechanics. But then what happens? They can't find work so they leave X and go elsewhere. At the same time, other students are studying business. They want to start companies and they need skilled workers. But it's difficult for companies to start up here. So they end up leaving too."

"Now, there's an alternative. The X Project. The X Project can help everyone here. It'll help young people start new companies in the area and help recently trained workers find jobs. We'll organise events to put employers in contact with employees. There'll be a web page and a data base. We'll introduce cost effective strategies for sharing office space, for buying materials in bulk at reduced prices, even co-hiring employees. By doing this, we can start a cycle of local employment. It's a self-propelling vision of the future. We just need some finance to get the ball rolling."

We just need some finance to get the ball rolling! Bloody hell, Richard thought. Nuria might have sounded a bit like a business manual but at that age, he couldn't recall having any 'self-propelling vision of the future.' I might have asked my father a few questions about economics, he thought. But creating a plan to actually change things for the better? That never crossed my mind.

"I can show you the site of the future X project offices," Nuria added. "If you like."

"You have that worked out too?" Richard replied.

"*Si*," she smiled. "It's just round the corner."

*

Fifteen minutes later, they were standing in front of a line of closed shops. "That was Dad's hardware store," Nuria said pointing to one of the graffiti-smothered shutters. "He ran it for fifteen years."

"What happened?"

"Bigger stores were built nearby. They got hold of cheaper goods so Dad couldn't compete. For years and years, he struggled on. But he wasn't making ends meet and the debt was slowly growing. When Mum died, he closed the place down."

"I'm sorry to hear about your Mum," Richard said.

Nuria shrugged.

"When did she pass away?"

"Two years ago."

"What does your Dad do now?"

"Nothing," Nuria replied. "Except sit at home, drink beer and watch TV."

She picked up a stone and threw it across the road. It rebounded off a closed shop shutter and clattered on the pavement. "If I win this competition," she said turning to Richard. "It'll give him hope. It'll show him that things aren't so bad. He can't spend the rest of his life like this, can he?"

The question wasn't rhetorical, Richard realised. It was more like a plea for help.

5
The Cycle of Life

Victor was sitting on a fallen trunk in the shade of a fig tree. He was reading a book on Buddhism. Trying to get to grips with the four noble truths: the truth of suffering, the truth of the arising of suffering, the truth of the cessation of suffering and the truth of the path leading to the cessation of suffering. He felt he understood number one but was having trouble working out the rest.

After a while, he closed the book and looked up. Elizabeth was walking towards him. The co-owner of Puerto Lobo looked relaxed in a khaki top, trousers and hiking boots. In the background, some of the children who had travelled with her, were laughing, splashing around in a pool by the stream. It was one of the pools Victor had dug the previous week. Now, a waterfall cascaded into it. Victor scratched his fluffy beard remembering how he hadn't believed that Ángel and Elizabeth's project would work.

"May I join you," Elizabeth asked.
"Of course," he replied moving up the trunk.
"Thank you," she said and sat down with a small sigh.
"I'm glad to have company," Victor offered.
Elizabeth studied Victor. "Are you really? You seem distant."

Victor knew she was speaking the truth. The community was different now. Estrella was gone, Gunne, Kristina and their kids were going back to Norway. The newcomers seemed happy together. They were younger than him and formed a tight-knit group. Plácido was around but he seemed busy.

"Things have changed here," he said.

"Things are always changing," Elizabeth said. "It's called the cycle of life."

"I guess so," Victor replied looking down at the book he had been reading. On the cover, the Buddha was sitting in the lotus position with his hands resting on his knees. The index finger and thumb on each hand, forming an O.

"Can I ask you something personal?" Elizabeth now said.

"Go ahead."

"Why did you come to Puerto Lobo?"

*

"So here I am," Victor said fifteen minutes later, when he had told Elizabeth his story. "Feeling a little lost again. Wondering if I should head to England to look for my biological parents or just return to Granada?"

"I never looked for my biological parents," Elizabeth said. "If that is what you like to call them."

Victor sat up. "You were adopted too?"

Elizabeth smiled. "I like to call it chosen. I was chosen by Ángel and Mabel. They were the most wonderful parents a child could have wished for. I have always felt so fortunate and loved. I know my brother Jaime, who is in Madrid, feels the same. We were blessed in a way, that out of the thousands of kids that must have been available at the time, they selected us."

Victor watched a child climb from a pool. "I thought I was blessed too. Now, I'm not so sure. Is that part of the cycle of life?"

Elizabeth laughed. "Most probably," she said. "Come on," she said placing the palms of her hands on the trunk. "Let's go and see Ángel."

6
It Could Have Been the Somme

"Where are we going?" Emily asked pulling the hood of her cagoule over her head as she left the Wellhouse building.

"Yeah," John said. "Where *are* we going? It's pissing down." He was wearing a cagoule too and Wellington boots. So were the others in the group.

"I told you it was a surprise," Katy replied, opening a gate.

"It had better be a good one," Lindsey Walsh muttered. "We've missed tea break."

Katy ignored that remark. Just let it go, she thought, you're not the target. Letting things go was part of her training. Since starting as a trainee care worker, she felt more positive. Like I have found a new direction, she told herself as she led the team down a muddy path. A fine mist floating down from the rolling hills. Giving everything a mystical beauty. As if we are lost in time, she mused.

They came to a slippery stile. "And trudged another mile," John sang. In fact, Katy stopped only twenty metres further on. Next to a strip of land marked out by a rope where some spades leaned against a wheelbarrow. Boxes of bulbs were stacked there too. Everyone gathered round.

"Ladies and gentleman," Katy said. "Welcome to the site of the new Wellhouse veg patch."

There was a moment's silence. Then Professor MacGregor took a tissue from one of his pockets and blew his nose. Lindsey Walsh muttered something. Katy had decided to say a few words so she pulled some notes out from a pocket. They were soggy.

She squinted, trying to read her own hand-writing. But the ink on the paper had run. Reminding her of the time she had flooded the kitchen in Fulham. She pictured herself bending down and picking a shopping list out of the water. Now she was trembling and it was no good anyway. So she put the piece of paper back in her pocket.

"Did you know that Doctor Bainbridge, the founder of the Wellhouse, studied Eastern medicine, philosophy and religion?" she asked.

"So bloody what!" Lindsey interrupted.

The others laughed. Katy coughed. Her eyes darted left and right. She felt green, a teacher in front of her first class. But she didn't run. She took a deep breath instead.

"Well, he liked the idea that a healthy body reflects a healthy mind," she said, her voice firmer now. "And he discovered the importance of a balanced diet. A diet of mainly fresh, organically grown fruit and vegetables. This has lots of benefits. It gives the body lots of vitamins and minerals. It provides fibre and helps us de-tox. It reduces the risk of heart disease and helps prevent some cancers. So instead of buying watery goods from other places, we're going to grow our own produce."

She paused here, and looked around. Blank faces mostly. Except Emily's. The skinny woman with wild hair nodded encouragingly.

"What's more, you get to work outside, in the fresh air," Katy continued. "The idea has been put to the board of governors and met with approval. The tools have been donated. All we need is a group of volunteers to make the project work. And I think you lot would be perfect."

Silence, again. Her would-be volunteers looked down or away. "I'm not sure if you quite understand the logistics of such a project Mrs. Brownlowe," Professor MacGregor said while adjusting his glasses. "Surely this is Gary Thompson's department?"

Katy shook her head. "Apparently not. He's busy keeping the rest of the garden and the grounds trim. But he has offered to help."

Lindsey Walsh stood smoking, in the rain. Her expression blank, her mouth turned down. "No fuckin' way," she said shaking her head. "Why should we do the dirty work?"

"It's for our benefit," Katy said.

"Is it?" Lindsey replied, throwing the cigarette to the ground. The end fizzled out. Then she turned and began to walk away. Others followed.

"Bloody slave labour," someone muttered.

Only Emily and John remained. Emily's eyes were gleaming. John pushed back the sleeves of his waterproof. "Can we start now?" he asked.

They each chose a spade and stood in a line on the edge of the strip of land. When Katy gave the signal, they started digging. There was relief on her face. Not exactly Waterloo, she thought, but it could have been the Somme.

7
What's Up?

It was Saturday morning and Richard was in the sitting room of his flat. He was wearing a dressing gown and fingerless gloves. He shifted his chair a little closer to the table and rubbed the stubble on his chin.

He was trying to write about his past but he wasn't sure where to start. At the beginning, I suppose. So he wrote about his earliest memories. About his childhood spent in a village in the south of England. He wrote about his mother and father, his grandparents and Moot, a gardener, whose leg had been blown off in a war. He wrote about his friends from the village and the school. He wrote about building camps and playing soccer and kissing a girl called Sophie.

Afterwards, he went to the bathroom. He took a good look in the mirror. And felt that the face staring back at him was different. Changed. Foreign somehow. All stubble and lines. Not the Richard Brownlowe who had lived in Fulham, London. Who had attended exhibition openings and dinner parties. He looked down at his hands gripping the edge of the sink. "Who exactly are you kidding?" he asked taking the gloves off and splashing water on his face.

*

In the afternoon, Richard went to the Albayzin. To see Mike. Since breaking up with Susie, Mike had quit teaching. He was unemployed, living in a van on a dead end street. When Richard arrived, he saw Boabdil lying curled up outside. But instead of rising in welcome, the wolf hound barely wagged its tail.

Richard knocked on the door of the van. Someone groaned from within. Eventually, Mike appeared, bare chested, wearing pyjama bottoms, shielding his eyes from the sun. "Oh, it's you," he said scratching his chin. "Come on in."

Inside, a stench of sweat and alcohol made Richard cringe. Flies buzzed around empty wine bottles and beer cans.

"Sorry about the mess," Mike muttered opening a window.

"I thought you were off booze," Richard said.

"Yeah," Mike grunted. "So did I."

They had tea seated on a wall next to the van. Richard noticed one of the van's tyres was flat but he didn't mention it. "So what's up?" he asked instead.

"What's up?" Mike repeated. "What's up? Nothing. Nothing is *up*. In fact, everything is down. Upside fucking down."

"How do you mean?"

"Susie's pregnant."

Richard's eyes widened in surprise.

Mike said: "The child is mine."

Richard scratched his head. He didn't know what to say. Mike must feel like he has gone back in time, he thought. When Mike's ex-wife became pregnant, they broke up. And now this. It explained why he was back on the booze.

"So what are you going to do?"

"Nothing. She wants the child but she doesn't want to be with me."

Afterwards, while walking back down through the Albaycin, Richard rang Susie. “I hear you’re pregnant,” he said. “Congratulations.”

“Congratulations? What is there to celebrate?”

“A new life.”

“I don’t think so.”

“Come on Susie. What about Mike?”

“I don’t want to talk about him,” she replied. Then she hung up.

8
Ángel

Victor and Elizabeth walked through the wild oak forest on the east side of Puerto Lobo. The old, gnarled trees on either side of the path giving shade. Victor remembering the time he had once collected wood with Estrella here.

As they approached the solitary cabin in a fenced off clearing, some dogs began barking. Then Ángel appeared. The sunlight shining off his white hair. As usual, he was dressed in an old grey suit and wore trainers on his feet. When he opened a gate, the dogs squeezed past him and ran up to Elizabeth. They were wagging their tails and whining in delight.

*

"Why don't you clear away some of that stuff Dad?" Elizabeth said. They were sitting down on the terrace of the cabin with glasses of lemonade. Elizabeth was referring to an old bath, a rusty fridge and some other junk lying in long weeds. Ángel shrugged. "You never know when it could come in useful."

"When could a rusty fridge come in useful?" Elizabeth asked.

"One day perhaps."

"And the old bath?"

"I don't know *hija*. There are many things I do not know."

Elizabeth smiled. "But there are some things you do know."

"Perhaps," he replied.

They talked for a while. Then Ángel and Elizabeth rose. Ángel wanted to show his daughter where he planned to put a generator. "In the meantime, you can make yourself useful *hijo,*" Ángel said to Victor. "And clear this stuff away."

"We won't be long," Elizabeth said with a wink.

Victor picked up an empty jug and the glasses and walked into the cabin. Inside, it was gloomy and dusty. The walls were decorated with old agricultural tools and framed black and white photographs. Victor put the jug and glasses by the sink and then looked more closely at the photos. In one, a group of well-dressed men sat on a bench. In another, some hunters stood on a hillside.

One photograph had been placed alone on a side table in the corner of the cabin. In it, two blonde kids were standing between a couple. It was Elizabeth and her brother, Jaime. The couple were Ángel and Mabel. Mabel had been the same height as Ángel but her hair was long and dark and her smile lit up her face.

*

"What happened to your mother?" Victor asked later, walking back along the path with Elizabeth.

"She was killed in a car accident."

"That must have been terrible," Victor said.

"It was," Elizabeth said. "One day she was with us and the next, she was gone. She had been the rock of our family."

Elizabeth smiled "Family and friends come and go Victor," she added. "They don't last forever so hold on to them while you can."

"The cycle of life again?" Victor wondered.

Elizabeth smiled. "Exactly," she said and hooked her arm through his.

After the visit to Ángel, Victor went back to his place. He sat down on a chair outside and looked down the valley while thinking about what Elizabeth had said.

9
Horder Road

When Katy left Dew cottage, she was emotional, trying to hide the tears as she strapped Toblerone's travel basket in the passenger seat of the Triumph. Meanwhile, James placed her suitcase and a box of books in the boot and Anne insisted she take some pre-prepared meals in a cooler bag. "There's a lasagne." she added.

Katy embraced her mother. Then her father. "I'll be in touch," she promised as she climbed into the driver's seat and started the engine. Waving as she drove away.

She took the A136 through Richmond. The traffic wasn't too bad. The soft top of the Triumph was down so the wind rushed through her hair. When Toblerone began meowing beside her, she said: "Not long now," and pressed her right foot harder down on the accelerator.

There was a space outside the house on Horder road. So she reversed into it. She had not been inside the house since she had left in the autumn. And was pleasantly surprised when she entered. The painting of the hall was complete; the carpet scrubbed, the newspapers and paint pots removed. In the kitchen, the smell of damp was barely noticeable. But she opened a window anyway, cringing slightly at the memory of the flood.

When she had unpacked, she held Toblerone and walked into the centre of the sitting room where she looked at all the stuff that had accumulated over time: the paintings, figurines, photographs, books, CDs, DVDs and board games.

The first objects she dropped in the bin were the wedding photographs. A set of Russian dolls was next. Followed by a lurid vase Richard liked and she had always found tasteless. Then she got a step ladder out from under the stairs and took the landscape that hung over the fireplace down.

It had been a present from Richard's parents. Two figures, on the right side of the canvas, were looking down a valley. They were standing side by side. She had always assumed they were a couple. Now, on closer inspection, she wondered if they weren't father and son.

10
Leonardo

Richard bit into a thin strip of roast beef. It was tender, melting in his mouth. "Delicious," he said to Tanya. The Assistant Director of Studies at the Newman School of English and her husband, José Pablo, were hosting the small lunch party. But Richard felt uncomfortable: Leonardo was a guest at the table too.

Out of the corner of his eye, Richard watched Leonardo pour himself another glass of wine. Then the Spaniard took out a cigar and tapped it on the surface of the table. He had been silent for most of the meal. As if he is working himself up for confrontation, Richard thought.

Richard put down his knife and fork, excused himself and rose. Because he had drunk too much Rioja, he walked unsteadily across the room. In the toilet, he came face to face with an image of Lord Kitchener. 'Briton Wants YOU!' Kitchener appeared to bellow. The image reminded Richard of his father and caused a jet of urine to splash over the edge of the ceramic bowl and onto the linoleum floor.

Afterwards, he flushed the toilet, washed his hands and opened the door. But his relief to be back out in the world was invaded by a new concern. There was Leonardo. Waiting outside the loo. Leaning against the wall. Puffing on his cigar. Thick smoke swirling in the air around him.

Richard tried to think of something to say. But no words came. None seemed appropriate. I don't blame him for loathing me, Richard thought. First, he loses a son. Then a wife. Now, the business is going down the drain. Leonardo stood straight. "*Eres un hijo de puta,"* the Spaniard whispered as he barged past Richard into the loo.

Richard walked unsteadily back to the table and sat down. Tanya smiled. José Pablo smiled. The other guests smiled too. Richard drank more wine.

*

The following day, while Richard was making coffee in the kitchen, the door bell rang. It was Leonardo.

"What do you want?" Richard asked through the intercom.

"To apologise," Leonardo replied.

When Leonardo entered the flat, Richard saw the Spaniard's hair was uncombed and there were shadows under his eyes. He was wearing the same clothes as the previous day but they were creased and a stain of red wine clouded the front of his shirt pink. An acid smell of body odour hung in the air. How the mighty have fallen, Richard thought wrinkling his nose, guessing that Leonardo had stayed up all night drinking.

They drank coffee sitting on the balcony of the flat. A swallow glided past. Below, a van rattled along the street. "This has been the worst year of my life," Leonardo said.

He glared at Richard. Face full of hate. Richard could almost feel the hate burning and he wondered whether Leonardo might suddenly rise and start laying into him again. But the Spaniard turned away. "I fucked up," he said.

Leonardo stayed the rest of the morning. He told Richard about a youth of endless *fiestas* and not much studying. Then, having failed to get a place at university, his parents had sent him away to study English.

"It was the first time I had ever been alone," he said. "I found a place to stay in Wimbledon and enrolled in a language school there. Fiona was my teacher. I fell in love with her but I didn't think I had a chance in hell of taking her out until we ended up together in a pub after an end of term party."

"Things continued from there. After my course ended, my father used his connections to get me a job in a company that specialised in Spanish imports. I immediately took to it, fitting in with my colleagues and making a success of things. Then one day, I proposed to Fiona and she accepted. We got married the following year."

"Those were good years," Leonardo said. Then he recounted what happened afterwards. The fact they had not been able to have children, the adoption of Victor, Leonardo losing his job, moving back to Spain, opening the language school.

"Things were still good. Everyone seemed happy. Then Fiona and I began drifting apart. I can't pinpoint when exactly. It just happened over time. Victor sensed it. Consciously or unconsciously, he sided with his mother. Life in the house became unbearable."

"That was when I started secretly dating a woman in Malaga. We weren't in love or anything and it didn't last. I just needed to escape and she needed a bit of company. Then Victor left."

"When I found you in Victor's room at the party, I thought something was up. So I followed you around. I saw you with Fiona and I blamed you for the fact that my life was falling apart. I could have killed you that night."

"And now?" Richard asked.

"Now I just feel numb," Leonardo replied raising his cup and taking a sip of coffee. "*Se acabo.* It's over."

11
Granada

Victor lifted his Alpine rucksack and swung it on to his back. Then he took a last look around the cabin. The bed was made, the chest of drawers bare. On a shelf, the book on Buddhism he had been reading, lay discarded beside a ferocious-looking clay troll that Knut, the oldest Norwegian kid, had made for him.

He walked down the path. Through a light mist which veiled the quiet valley. He could hear bird song, the running stream and a breeze rustling the leaves of the trees. Plácido was waiting in the clearing. Poking some smouldering ashes from the previous night's fire with a stick.

"Ready?" he asked.

"As ready as I'll ever be."

"Let's go then."

They walked out of the camp and then down the track which ran through the pine forest. A light rain began to fall. Victor rubbed his beard. He felt calm inside. "How's it going with Meiko" he asked, thinking of the Japanese girl Plácido was dating.

"Not bad at all," Plácido said.

"How long will she be here?"

"Until the summer."

"Then what?"

"Then she goes back to Japan."

"Will you visit?"

"Maybe," Plácido said.

When the two men got to the village, they sat on the terrace of the only restaurant. Sunlight shining on the church that stood on the edge of a square. The waiter came over and they ordered breakfast. Victor choosing *churros con chocolate*. Plácido going for a more rural, Spanish breakfast: toast with tomato and ham and a coffee. Then rolling a cigarette and leaning back to smoke it. The wind blowing the smoke south.

"We met here," Plácido said. "Do you remember?"

"How could I forget?" Victor replied, with a smile.

Plácido laughed. "Are you glad you came?"

Victor nodded. "Puerto Lobo isn't an easy place to live in but it's certainly not boring. You never know what's going to happen from one day to the next."

"That's for sure."

"I might have lost Estrella but I made good friends. And I sorted my head out. I feel ready to go back."

"You're a wiser kid now," Plácido said. He took another drag of his cigarette. "So you're going back to college?"

"If they'll have me."

"They'll have you," Plácido said.

It wasn't long before the coach to Granada arrived. Victor put his luggage in the hold. And then embraced Plácido. Plácido slapped him on the back. The men wishing each other luck. Then Victor boarded. And found a window seat at the back. As the coach pulled away, he waved to his friend who stood by the side of the road.

The coach rumbled away. It headed east. Through Lanjarón and then it crossed the Tablate bridge and turned north. Onto the dual carriageway. Chugging up hill. Then it picked up speed again and approached the city.

Victor looked through the window. High rise flats, hotels, shops, traffic. In the bus station, he disembarked and collected his luggage. He was feeling uneasy. Surrounded by the din and chaos of the city. Wondering whether he was ready to return home.

The city bus he boarded, barged its way through dense traffic into the centre of town. Victor alighted in Puerta Real. Then walked down La Carrera de la Virgen, passing the Cortes Inglés and the church of our Lady of Sorrows. The leaves of the huge plane trees hung glistening after some rain. Down by the river, swifts and swallows raced through the sky. New arrivals, Victor thought, like me.

My parents must be at work, Victor deduced when he arrived at 37 Acacia Street. The shutters were down. He walked to the café bar to get the spare set of keys. Miguel, the owner, did not recognise him at first. I must look like a bum, Victor thought.

Inside the house, he knew something was up. Because there was a cigar in an ashtray on the table in the hall. Something Fiona would not normally permit. He went into the kitchen and found a yellowed note on the table:

Dear Victor,
Welcome home.
Please stay.
Love Dad

He went upstairs and into his parents' bedroom. The bed was unmade. Some of Leonardo's clothes lay on the back of a chair. He opened the doors of his mother's wardrobe. It was empty except for a row of coat hangers whose jingle-jangle broke the silence.

12
Flying

Katy cradled a mug of coffee while she looked out the kitchen window at a lone cluster of daffodils in the corner of the patio garden. But she wasn't really thinking about the flowers or spring. She was thinking about Victor. She couldn't help it.

After turning away from the window, she put the mug down on the table beside her lap top. The screen showed a training course unit entitled Hospital Care. But she could not concentrate fully. Victor was niggling her. He was clawing his way through her mind.

*

She chose a window seat on the train she boarded at Clapham Junction. And watched grimy houses and office blocks flash by. Then a park and a wood. Then more offices and houses. She bit a nail and wondered if she was doing the right thing. When she had told her parents, they tried to dissuade her from going. But she hadn't listened to them.

When the train pulled into Gatwick, she hurried through the hustle and bustle of the train station and airport check in.

Through customs. A cup of coffee in departures. Browsing in a couple of shops. Then boarding the plane. Still biting her nails. Still wondering if she was doing the right thing.

The last time I flew, she remembered, Richard and I went to Paris. To celebrate our fifth anniversary. It had been an attempt at rekindling their marriage. As if a holiday could make a difference. But it had been a disaster. Katy remembered feeling incredibly tired as Richard dragged her through the city. All she had wanted to do was sit. Or lie down. But of course that had not been possible. In a restaurant, she had barely touched her meal and he had exploded. Blown his top. And walked out.

She didn't blame him at the time. For not understanding. But now? She shook her head and looked out of the window. At scattered clouds. And a parched mountain range below. She thought of some lines of Lorca's. How did they go? Something about a mountain, a shepherd and bitter weeds. There was a child. And sharp thorns on a hill. She closed her eyes. She didn't want to think any more.

In Malaga bus station, she sat on a bench and watched life going by: the Alsina Graelles coaches arriving and departing with shudders and groans, the passengers getting on and getting off, friends and families chatting and bickering, and she wondered if she would ever be a part of it. Part of this thing called life. And not just a spectator, like someone who wanders around an exhibition. But is somehow detached from what is happening around her.

13
Flown

"Mike!" Richard called out, stooping in the doorway of the van. But there was no reply. The interior of the vehicle was a mess. Empty beer cans lay strewn on the table. The sink was piled high with unwashed plates. Flies rose from the open bin. Richard putting his hand over his mouth to stifle the stench.

He found Mike's wolf hound shivering in a corner. Staring vacantly out. Fur lank and crusted with dirt. "What's the matter Boab?" he asked stretching out a hand to stroke the dog. The dog growled, then snapped.

Afterwards, Richard approached one of Mike's neighbours, who was working on the engine of a vehicle parked in the street, and asked if Mike was around. The man picked up a rag and wiped his oily hands.

"I've haven't seen him for a couple of days."

"He left the dog?"

The man nodded. "Strange, isn't it?"

After that, Richard walked back through the Albaycin. Using the shade offered by the high walls of the villas. Sprawling ivy, prowling cats. Someone was playing a *bulería*. He couldn't believe Mike had just upped sticks and left, abandoning the dog. Despite what the man was going through.

In a small square, a figure was curled up on a bench, wearing a moth eaten coat. There was a smashed guitar lying in pieces beside him. Richard approached but it wasn't Mike. The man's face was olive green, the skin marked by a series of scars. In his withered left hand, he clasped a wooden cross.

Back in the flat, Richard sat on the terrace with a cool beer. Watching the swifts and swallows speeding across the sky. Still wondering where Mike had flown. Another missing person. Another lost soul. Wandering alone. Like Victor. Like Katy. Like Fiona. Like Leonardo. Like me?

A car passed below. Its tyres squealing on candle wax; a leaving present from a procession that had passed earlier that morning. He took a swig of beer. A gecko appeared. He watched it climbing along the wall. The peculiar head and beady eyes. Its thin body and feet. Not far away, he could hear the beat of drums. And then a blast of trumpets. Incense wafted on a breeze. Coming from the river.

14
The Procession

Victor was caught up in the crowd, watching the masked *penitents*. Dressed in purple robes, the cones on their heads, pointing to the sky. A grimacing Christ on a cross on a candle lit canopy. Wearing a crown of thorns. Blood dripping down the side of his face.

When the drums stopped, the procession halted. Some beefy, bare-chested bearers came out from underneath the canopy. They were wearing woollen hats. Support belts strapped round their stomachs. Other men took their places. The canopy was lifted again to applause. The procession moved on. The drummers drummed out the rhythm. The horns played. The band marched by.

Behind the band came the grieving women. In black dresses. The lace on their headpieces trailing down their backs. They stood straight and proud, holding candles. Wax dripping onto the road or onto the balls of wax held by squatting kids.

More *penitents* went by. Then came soldiers. Marching in formation. Some official looking members of the church followed dressed in purple robes. A statue of the virgin came after them.

She sat mournfully on a canopy with golden tassels. She was wrapped in a heavy, delicately embroidered cape. She was surrounded by flowers, candles and silver bars. Tears fell down her cheeks. Behind her, came another brass band.

A man dressed in overalls followed the procession. Carrying a step ladder and cleaning materials.

Victor crossed the road and headed to the Newman School of English. In the park, in front of the school, the leaves on the orange trees glistened. A crisp packet floated in the murky water of a fountain. Victor went up the steps and pushed open the door of the school. In an empty reception, light illuminated the cigar smoke which wafted from the office.

Victor approached silently. Leonardo was hunched over the desk, asleep, his head cradled in his arms. A cigar smouldered in an ashtray. A mug of coffee. A photograph. Victor stared at the photograph. He was dressed in a school uniform. Fresh faced and smiling. He frowned and rubbed his beard. Trying to recall that boy. But he couldn't for the life of him.

15
Acacia Street

Katy perched on a stool in the hotel restaurant. Eating toast smothered in tomato pulp and olive oil. Drinking fresh orange juice. The bits swirling in her glass. She hadn't been able to sleep. It had been too warm in the room. And she hadn't been able to turn the heating down. Now, she felt tired. But it was a care free tiredness. One that she didn't mind owning. There would be time for sleep later, she knew.

After breakfast, she left the hotel and walked over to the first taxi in a line on the street outside. When she showed the driver the address, he nodded.

The taxi went slowly through the centre of town. Past the cathedral. It stopped at a traffic light in front of a statue of Columbus. He was offering the keys of the New World to Queen Isabel.

They went down Reyes Católicos. Passing the designer shops. Then Acera del Darro with its cafés and restaurants. And Cortes Inglés. Down to the river.

She paid the driver and got out on the corner of Acacia street. Approaching number 37 quietly. Hands in the pockets of her jacket. When she arrived, she stood on the pavement beside the mimosa tree, opposite the house. And saw a young man sitting at the table on the patio. He was reading a book. A jasmine entwined a railing beside him. Its white flowers out. Their aroma wafting on a breeze.

Katy stood very still. Her heart beating hard against her chest. As if it would break out. Is that really Victor? she asked herself. Unable to believe it. Wondering why Richard hadn't told her.

Leave, she told herself. But she couldn't pull herself away. Instead, she found herself crossing the road. And standing outside the gate. Watching Victor and thinking: after all this time.

She just stood there gazing at him. They were divided only by the gate. She ran a hand through her hair. And controlled her breathing. Her heart beat slowed. She was a little calmer. Perhaps Richard did tell me, she thought, but I deleted the email. Perhaps he doesn't know. It doesn't matter now.

She wondered what Victor would say when she introduced herself. But he didn't look up. And she didn't leave.

ACKNOWLEDGEMENTS

A big Thank You goes to family and friends for their support and patience. A special thanks go to Loida, Will, Darius, Tom and Sam. I would also like to thank Martin Ouvry, Margaret James, the Granada Writers' Club and the team at Circulo Rojo.